THE BRIDE DINED ALONE

THE BRIDE DINED ALONE

Vera Kelsey

COACHWHIP PUBLICATIONS
Greenville, Ohio

First published 1943
Audrey Vera Kelsey, 1892-1961
CoachwhipBooks.com

ISBN 1-61646-558-1
ISBN-13 978-1-61646-558-2

1

Friday Evening, July 25

Just at the hour when quiet held the evening like a cup the message arrived.

Chang brought word of it to the open veranda where Mother and Dad Madison sat silently side by side in the rocking swing, watching the light change over lawns and apple orchards and on the varied greens of the woods beyond.

Daphne, their daughter-in-law, sat on the step. In her fresh pink play suit, her dreamy eyes fixed on a spray of sunset-touched cloud high in the paling sky, she looked all of twelve years old. Above her, hands in pockets, lounged Dock, her husband, eyes on her.

The old Chinese stood behind them a moment, his face impassive, looking, too, at that tangible peace. Not a leaf stirred. Not a bird called. Trees, petunias, the bright masses of color lining Phlox Walk, the very grass seemed conscious of the stillness in which day merged with night.

He looked from one to the other of the family he had served so long and loyally. Mother Madison, ample and gentle and faded, in a blue-sprigged cotton dress. Dad Madison, so tall and thin and frail, it appeared a breath of wind from the north could shrivel and blow him away like an autumn leaf.

Quietly, almost carefully, as if he knew his words would shatter more than the peace of that hour, Chang said, "Telephone, Missy Martha. Belong cable."

All four turned to look at him. Before the complete impassivity of his face their common surprise changed to concern, then alarm.

Dock spoke quickly and moved quickly for so large a young man. "Sit still, Mother. I'll take it."

He was gone a long time. The others waited with growing uneasiness, their eyes on the view before them. Already it seemed different. A breeze was stirring the tips of elms and maples. Though its breath was scented with phlox and petunias, it now seemed hot, oppressive. Robins, encouraged by the stillness, rustled round from the south lawns in search of their evening worms. A few, bolder than the rest, or perhaps sensing in advance the coming desertion of the house, ventured almost to the step on which Daphne sat.

Turning impatiently, she put them all into short flights to safer zones. Her heart-shaped face, framed in dark hair, was set and cold. Her dark eyes, too, were cold.

"It's Dana, of course," she said. "I knew these past two years were too good to be true. We've been so free—so safe, and sane and happy. Now she's coming back to spoil everything."

"Hush, Daphne." Mother Madison's eyes turned anxiously on her husband. "If she were coming home she'd write. Maybe there's some mistake. Dana wouldn't telegraph—cable—from Bogota."

"She'd use a rocket ship if she could—just to be different." Daphne jumped up. "What's keeping Dock? I'll go—"

"Wait," Dad Madison advised quietly. "He's coming now." And they could hear Dock's long strides crossing the floor of the living room behind them. Screens of the double doors burst outward as he arrived, one hand full of papers.

He sent an enigmatic glance at his wife before he turned to his parents in the swing. "Wish I had the money these represent," he said. "Make a neat nest egg."

Sitting down, he began to jostle the papers into alignment. Dad and Mother Madison remained silent, eying him expectantly. But Daphne couldn't wait. "What is it?" she prodded.

"Dana. A cable. She's arriving Sunday night—with a new husband. Chap named"—to cover the quick and different silence that fell round him he fumbled with the papers—"Carter Coyne. She wants her house opened and everyone to have dinner there Sunday night. They expect to reach New York tomorrow morning by plane. Will remain overnight and Sunday. Then drive out—"

"Drive out!" Dad smiled. "Dana must think gas rationing a new figure of speech."

"What else does she say?" Mother Madison's voice was calm, deliberately placid.

The young doctor's good-natured face crinkled around the eyes with amusement. "Well, I've four pages of words here, but that's about all she says. Except that this Carter Coyne has to see a number of people in New York and she, of course, is in rags—simply must shop. We dine, I gather," he concluded ironically, "at eight and are thus nicely assembled for her big entrance, whenever it pleases her to make it."

He offered the papers to his mother, looked at his wife. Daphne had remained explosively still where she stopped when he began to speak. Now she broke out in two words packed with distaste and resentment.

"Married again!"

"Married again" was obviously the thought in all their minds. The others were silent, considering it.

"Carter Coyne," Dad mused after a time. "That name's familiar somehow. Seems to me I read—"

"I thought so too, Dad." Dock rose. "Got your last Sunday's *Times* handy?"

"That's it. That's where I read—" Dad Madison sat forward, startled. "But this can't be the Carter Coyne Dana's married. He's the fellow that cleaned up ten million or billion on tin—maybe manganese—some war material down there."

"Can't be! That's just the man she would marry!" Daphne spun round on her husband. "And do you know what we're going to do? We're moving."

"Well, now, Daph, I don't see any call for you to do that," Dad protested mildly. "Isn't likely this Carter Coyne's the sort of man to be content long in a quiet country place like this."

"That won't matter to Dana," his daughter-in-law declared. "She'll start revamping our homes before she takes off her hat. Our house is too big as it is. So is yours. You and Dock know how hard it is for Mother and me to manage with just one servant. Heaven knows what she'll do to them now she has millions to play with."

"I'm afraid we can't move before Sunday night." Dock smiled up at his irate little wife. "I do have a few patients, you know. And the poison-ivy season's reaching a peak in these parts. I think the goldenrod's going to do well by me too."

"It's easy for you to laugh—you and Dad," Daphne stormed on. "You don't care what people say—and think. But Mother and I do. We don't enjoy having our homes pointed out as monuments to Dana's progressively rich husbands! I'd sooner be back in the shack we made out of Dad's old shed when we were married than in that Long Island country place we've got now."

She flung a contemptuous glance toward the long, winged, white house outlined against the green woods to the north. "I hate it—every foot of it!"

"You've actually seen someone drive up Madison Farms Road to point at our homes?" Dock teased. "That relieves my mind. I've always intended when I had time to see if there weren't signs posted somewhere, 'Road Closed. Pestilence Ahead.'"

"It isn't the house you hate, Daphne," Mother Madison corrected. "You know we were all more comfortable and pleased, too, when Dana first started changing things after Fretz died. It's because she used Blake Amery's money for the new additions you hate, dear. You must be fair."

"Fretz Dreier was different," Daphne conceded. "I didn't mind having his money change our shack into a cottage. But that white elephant!" Again she waved contemptuously toward her own home. "And this one of yours! You shouldn't have sold her the Farms, Dad, when Blake died. That's when the trouble started."

"Dad didn't sell her everything," Dock reminded. "He still has ten acres. So have we. And it did seem reasonable when she was remodeling her own home to let her do ours. You were just as keen as she was, remember, not to have ours look like the super—like a gatehouse."

He interrupted himself hastily to pull Daphne down on the arm of his chair. "Take it easy, petrel. I wouldn't miss this arrival for—well, anything I could offer would be peanuts now in comparison with millions. Dana put on a pretty good show when she came back with Blake—"

Again he stopped, turned apologetically to his mother. "Sorry. I shouldn't have said that."

"Why not say it?" Daphne demanded. "Married three times in eight years! Disgusting! Oh, not the marriages. I wouldn't mind—I'd be glad—if she married because she loved someone. But she loves Rick. These others—just for money—and a name in the news—"

Mother Madison was not listening. Neither she nor Dad had said a word about the new marriage. Now they were reading the scribbled sheets together slowly and in silence.

At length she looked up, troubled. "Dana says she's sending servants out from New York. Her husband's arranging for them. Except for a butler. She wants Bixby to see if he can get Stewart for her again. And she wants him to measure her north field. What field does she mean?" She looked out toward the woods circling the north.

Daphne's face brightened. "I've changed my mind, Dock. We're staying. Just to see Dana's face when she discovers her 'Superintendent Bixby' hasn't done a thing she wanted. What she'll say when she sees Pelleas and Melisande!"

"I knew there'd be a silver lining in this somewhere," Dad drawled. "This will be the end of that fellow—"

"I hope you've kept all those phony weekly reports he's turned in," Dock said.

"Every one."

"Oh, he'll get around her someway—just as he always has—about the Farms." Daphne's feathers ruffled again. "It's Pelleas and Melisande I'm counting on. She adores those two pools."

"Hist!" Dock warned melodramatically. "Speak of the devil—"

2

Friday Evening, July 25

A large, heavily built man in rough, outdoor clothing and high-laced boots was cutting across the north lawn from Phlox Walk toward them. In one hand fluttered a square of blue paper.

"Evening, folks," he greeted them familiarly while still several yards away.

No one answered until he reached the step. Dad Madison rose slowly. "Good evening, Bixby."

He walked with careful steps across the veranda to receive the delft-blue square. "I'll just read it over so we'll all know what you've done this week." His light, almost weak voice had an edge.

The heavy face darkened, but Bixby said nothing.

"'Monday, July 28, mowed Doc Madison's lawns,'" Dad read aloud.

"'Tuesday, July 29, sprayed Dad Madison's west orchard—'"

The superintendent's hand moved to recover the report, but Dock anticipated him. With a stride he reached his father's side. Taking the report, he regarded it with lively interest.

"July 28!" he exclaimed. "Why, that's next Monday, Bixby. So now you're mowing my lawns in the future! Well, that's more than you've ever done in the past."

"Mistake," the man mumbled. "That's part of my memo for next week. My daughter typed it with this week's report. Mixed them up, I guess."

"How is it different from any other report you've ever turned in?" Daphne demanded scornfully. "You know you've never done one thing on Dad Madison's place or ours, Bixby, though my sister expects and pays you to care for them."

Bixby's head went back sharply, and his voice, too, wore an edge. "Can't be in three places at once, Mrs. Dock. Though I do get around." He turned, his manner more respectful, to say, "Yes, Mrs. Madison?"

"You won't need to bring these reports to us any more, Bixby. Mrs. Coyne is returning Sunday night." At his expression she explained calmly, "My daughter Dana has just married again. She is now Mrs. Carter Coyne. She is coming home Sunday night, and I have some messages for you."

His low but penetrating whistle interrupted her. "Carter Coyne, eh?"

"She wants you to locate Stewart again if you can and to measure her north field. I'm to telephone the measurements to her in New York at noon tomorrow."

The man's small black eyes flickered like flies over them all. For some obscure reason he seemed to find satisfaction, even pleasure, in the cold resentment for him they made no effort to conceal.

"Any idea what for?" he asked.

Daphne ignored her husband's restraining glance to break in angrily: "It's none of your business, Bixby. Mrs. Coyne will tell you herself when she wants you to know. And I hope she tells you something else—"

"Don't bother your little head, Mrs. Dock." Bixby's smooth insolence was maddening. "There's no north field to measure. And I've been thinking myself I was about due to retire. Maybe I will—now."

Without a word he turned and strode back the way he had come, whistling to himself. Silently, almost incredulously, they watched him go.

"You think he means that?" Dad asked. "I don't. He's got the softest job on the planet here and he knows it. He'll never give it up—"

"Maybe he'll have to—without any help from us," Dock suggested cryptically. Their unanimous expectancy overcame his judgment. "He's been talking too much—as usual. Spreading rumors that defense stamps are counterfeit, that the rich are exempt from the draft. The FBI's going to get him if he don't watch out."

"One way or another he's got to go," Mother Madison declared. She nodded toward a lawn bordering Phlox Walk, where a governess moved from bed to bed of flowers while two small charges, a boy and a girl in pajamas and light, flying bathrobes, fluttered about like butterflies. "Dana may not care what happens to the Farms, but she does love her children. She can get another superintendent but never another governess like Mademoiselle."

"Bix still making life miserable for her?" Dock's eyes as he spoke were following the darting seven-year-old boy with an odd concern.

Mother Madison nodded. "He's invented a new way to—to force her to be nice to him. When she won't accept his invitations he takes out his displeasure on his daughter. What can Mademoiselle do? She is very fond of Mary. She's always loathed Bixby, but now I think she's really afraid of the man." She turned to look again at the trio on the lawn. Daphne, turning, too, sprang up. "Dock!" she exclaimed in concern. "Look! Perhaps you'd better go."

They all turned then to see that the governess, a tall, slender woman, was alone on Phlox Walk. Too late to retreat as she saw Bixby approaching, she had stepped aside, almost into the flowers, to permit him to pass.

But Bixby showed no sign of passing. He stopped, was speaking rapidly to her. As they watched her head went back incredulously; her whole body stiffened. She remained motionless, offering no reply to whatever he was saying to her.

"The beast! Dock, go—" Daphne urged.

"Sit still," Dad said, and there was a smile in his voice. "Here come Whiffles and Bunny to the rescue."

Across the lawns toward Phlox Walk from the left, seven-year-old Whiffles was racing headlong, rage evident in his waving arms. From the other side, straight through the phlox, burst another storm center. Sturdy, squarish, three-year-old Bunny.

Pausing only to seize one of Mademoiselle's hands, she took a solid stance, thrust up a small but defiant chin, opened her mouth, and left it that way. The result was a roar that drowned out Whiffles' breathless shouts as he arrived to support Mademoiselle on the other side.

The combination obviously was too much even for Bixby. With an angry shake of his heavy shoulders he moved on up the walk.

Mademoiselle stood a moment, tightly holding the protecting hands grasping hers. Then swiftly she dropped to her knees and drew both children into her arms. The intensity of her emotion was evident to the group watching from the veranda. They looked at one another in mutual concern and understanding.

"He was telling her!" Daphne's voice, low now, was full of sympathy and apprehension. "He told her Dana's coming home. I know it."

Dad sighed. "Well, someone had to tell her. Perhaps it's just as well Bixby did it. She's going to be upset. Sometimes lately it's been difficult to realize the children are Dana's—not hers. Especially Whiffles."

"It's going to be hard for them to realize it too," Mother Madison said unhappily. "Maybe it's all for the best Dana's coming home."

Dock nodded, his eyes still intent on the trio on Phlox Walk. The governess had moved to a low white seat in the midst of the flowers, and all three sat there in some silent communion, the children pressed close to her on either side.

"Have you ever thought, Mother," Dock asked carefully, "that it might be a good idea for Dana to find another Mademoiselle?" He smiled wryly. "No one around Dana ever seems to do anything in moderation. Bixby does less than nothing. Mademoiselle more than enough. I know I wouldn't want our boys exposed to that emotional care twenty-four hours a day."

"Your savages!" Dad scoffed fondly. "Can you imagine them going round every evening before bedtime to say good night to the flowers?"

Dock laughed, then was serious. "No, but I can imagine something else. I can imagine Whiffles and Bunny flying to the defense of Mademoiselle against Dana just as they did now against Bixby. And you know how Dana will react to that."

"We're all forgetting," Mother Madison reminded them, "that even if Mademoiselle wished to go she couldn't—under the terms of Fretz' will."

"Unfortunately Fretz' will and Dana's are two different things," Dock commented dryly. "If she discovers this complication between Mademoiselle and Bixby—" He shrugged. "Dana didn't take lightly Blake Amery's interest in the lady, if you remember."

Chang had arrived in the doorway while Dock was speaking. Now he stepped out to announce dinner.

"Missy Dana come home?" he asked. "She wanchee Stewart? No get him. War get him." He smiled all round with satisfaction.

"Oh, dear," Mother Madison said, rising. "Then we'll have to go over first thing in the morning, Chang."

"I'll send Bertha to help," Daphne offered without enthusiasm, then capitulated with a smile for Mother Madison. "Oh well, I'll come too. But this is the last time."

She stopped, turned slowly, listening. They were all listening. Clearly on the evening air came the notes of a violin. A violin responding to the bow of a master hand.

Dad Madison sighed. "Poor Rick!"

"Poor Dana!" Dock corrected. "She can't know he's Hedrick now."

"Not know Hedrick!" Daphne exclaimed. "War or no war, the whole world knows Hedrick."

Understanding flashed in her eyes. She shivered as the sound of arpeggios rippling from the strings grew clearer.

"Let's go in," she urged hastily.

3

Sunday Evening, July 27

Their silent dinner in Dana's summer dining room over, Dad and Mother Madison, followed by Dock and Daphne, sought the wide, stone-laid terrace on the east end of the house. Wearily they sank into the cushioned chairs there and welcomed Chang with coffees on a tray.

"And a highball for me, Chang," Dock said, taking his. "When I say high, I mean high."

"For me too," echoed his wife. "The dinner was elegant, Chang." As the Chinese departed she added, "But I ate it with my ears and listened with my tummy. What do you recommend for suspense, darling? It's killing me."

"Sweet words." Dock's long fingers laced themselves among the curls caught in a topknot on her head, tilted her flushed face upward. "You look super-duper sweet in that long skirt, woman. Long time since I've seen you in dinner clothes."

Dad Madison permitted himself a mild snort. "Dinner clothes! You're married to a farmer's son, Daph, my dear. Remember that." He looked complacently from his loose, worn white suit to his wife's freshly laundered summer dress. "If you can't make up your own minds, dress up to the Madisons, not the—the Coynes."

"You've got something there, Dad," Dock agreed. "Dinner jackets in July. Whew! I'd sooner have poison ivy."

Daphne surveyed her tall husband with shining eyes, then winked at Dad. "A farmer's son implies a farm, Dad darling. Look around you."

She waved a hand toward the landscaped and meticulously groomed grounds. Lawns as smooth and green as softest silk rippled off on all sides. Symmetrically placed gardens of roses and shrubs, towering, well-cared-for oaks and elms and firs broke them into charming, intimate vistas and combined to conceal all three homes from the road.

Two long vivid lines of color—Phlox Walk to the south, linking Dana's grounds with Dad and Mother Madison's, and Dahlia Walk to the west, linking Dana's grounds with those of Dock and Daphne—accented their triangular form. Beyond the artfully placed trees to the west also lay a low boundary wall and Madison Farms Road. North, east, and south, the lawns were circled by orchards of apple, pear, and cherry trees. Beyond them rolled the darkening wall of woods.

"It's lovely—gorgeous—wonderful," Daphne admired, looking at Dad. "But is it a farm?"

Dad merely smiled, refusing to be drawn. Dock broke the silence with a laugh. "That's right, Dad. Ignore her. She knows very well the Farms are just where they've always been—east of the woods. At that, the woman may have the right idea. What she can't see doesn't exist for her. Bless you, Chang." He rose to lift two highball glasses from the tray, gave one to Daphne.

"Drink her down, honey. The big scene's due any minute now."

"What is it, Chang?" Mother Madison asked as the Chinese turned to her.

"Cook, she come now, Missy Martha. More better I go."

"So the cook's a she," Dad deduced.

Mother Madison, understanding Chang's opinion of women cooks, nodded her consent for Chang to leave but smiled to herself. He would not go, she knew, until he had welcomed Dana home personally, made sure everything was in order for her.

When Chang disappeared inside she answered her husband. "Evidently. I was expecting a man, too, from the name—Sardaki. Well, that's eight. They're all here now except the chauffeur, who'll drive them out, and a butler. Mademoiselle will have to run the house until Dana can find one."

Dock and Daphne glanced at one another, broke into howls of laughter.

"Eight here and two to come—or go!" Daphnc gasped finally. "And just eight years ago this house was a barn!"

Her laughter died quickly. "And your living room now, Dad, was your whole farmhouse then. Oh, I wish we were back in those days when Dana married Fretz and we were all so busy painting and hammering we didn't have time—"

"Those were the days!" Dock seconded heartily. "We were the busiest, carefree-est crowd in all New York State. Fretz was a fine fellow, even if he was an etymologist or entomologist—I never can get that word straight. Remember, Dad, the time we had to dump a whole load of hay to let him find that new beetle?"

"I remember better that whenever I needed either of you," Dad answered dryly, "you had to rush off to feel a pulse and Fretz to tail a butterfly or something—"

He stopped. They all fell silent, remembering the day Fretz followed a butterfly so heedlessly and never returned.

Daphne's matter-of-fact mind turned to practical channels. "I know what Dana meant by the north field," she announced after a time. "She meant the north woods. I remember hearing her say she wanted Bixby to clear them out while she was away. And she wanted a bridge built over Pelleas and Melisande so that—so that it couldn't happen again."

Dad Madison moved irritably. "Dana and you and Dock grew up here, Daph, played everywhere. Did anything ever harm you—or Mother or me? Bunny and Whiffles play outside all day long. So do your youngsters. And Mother and you are in and out of the woods every summer, picking blueberries. Outside of a garter snake or two, have you ever met a snake—a poisonous snake?"

"Give some credit to Bessie," Dock interjected. "Any of you seen her lately? I caught a glimpse of her a few days ago, slithering along one of the woods paths. Business must be good. I'll bet she's five feet long now, if she's an inch, and fat as butter."

"She's a beauty!" Dad beamed with approval. "And worth her weight in gold. Knows her place too. Never comes on the lawns herself, but neither does anything else."

"Then you admit there's something to come," Daphne pointed out.

Dock stirred uncomfortably. "Think we ought to warn this new addition to the family to beware the woods?"

"I've been thinking about that too, Dad," Mother Madison said uneasily. "Even if there's no danger for us, it would be awful—"

"Dana will tell him about Fretz and Blake," Dad assured her.

"She didn't tell Blake about Fretz," Daphne reminded him.

"You couldn't tell Blake anything, if you remember," Dock broke in. "The idea of a city feller like him going into those woods alone, anyway. If it hadn't been for Bixby we never would have found him."

"Poor little Dana!" Mother Madison murmured sadly. "To have that happen twice."

Dock asked quickly, "Well, what's the decision? Do we or don't we warn Carter Coyne that these woods aren't healthy for Dana's husbands?"

"Dock!" His wife turned shocked eyes on him.

"I'm sorry." Dock was sincerely contrite. "That sounded worse than I meant—"

"Listen!" Mother Madison rose, turned toward the screen doors behind them. Inside they could hear Chang's voice saying, "Welcome home, Missy Dana."

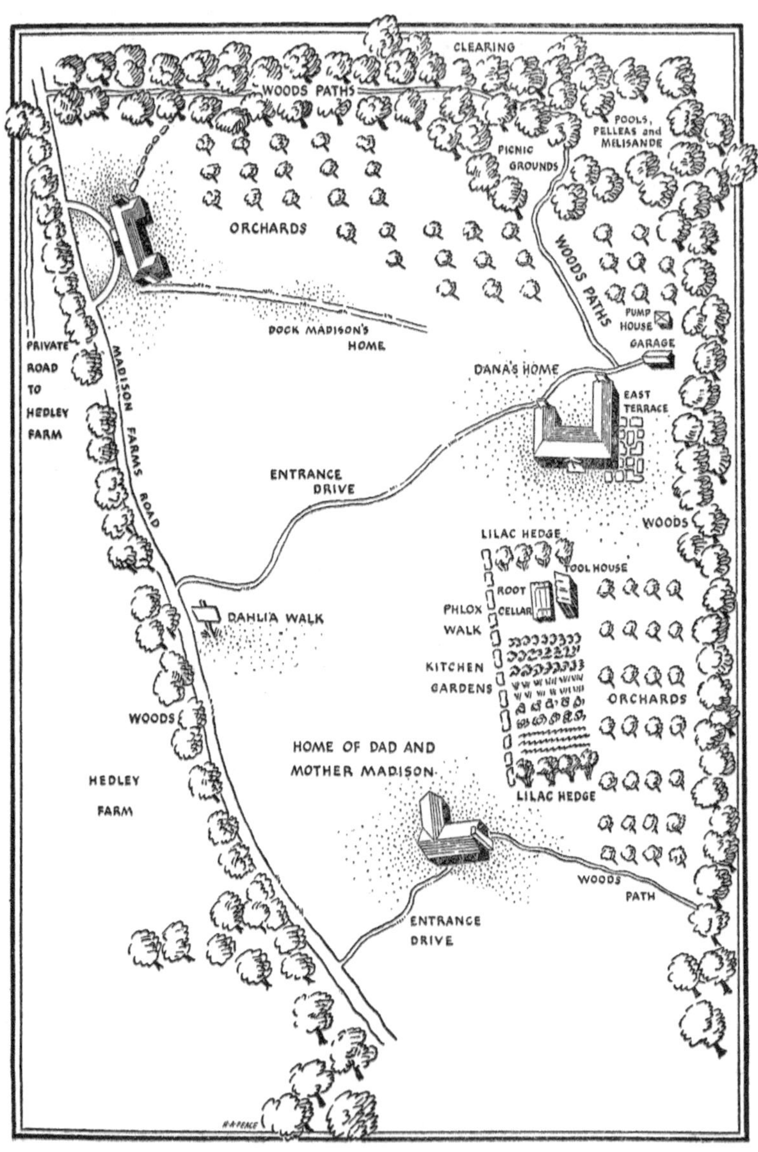
CLEARING
WOODS PATHS
POOLS, PELLEAS and MELISANDE
PICNIC GROUNDS
ORCHARDS
WOODS PATHS
PUMP HOUSE
GARAGE
DOCK MADISON'S HOME
PRIVATE ROAD TO HEDLEY FARM
MADISON FARMS ROAD
DANA'S HOME
EAST TERRACE
ENTRANCE DRIVE
WOODS
LILAC HEDGE
TOOL HOUSE
ROOT CELLAR
PHLOX WALK
DAHLIA WALK
KITCHEN GARDENS
ORCHARDS
WOODS
HOME OF DAD AND MOTHER MADISON
LILAC HEDGE
HEDLEY FARM
WOODS PATH
ENTRANCE DRIVE

4

Sunday Evening, July 27

Before Mother Madison could reach the doors Dana appeared. She stood a moment, framed against the lights behind her. A lovely Dana, revealing, even in silhouette, an exciting, gaunt chic. The light gleamed on her blond hair, simply, shrewdly simple, in smooth rolls framing her slender face.

Suddenly the gray cocktail suit of crepe or chiffon, with mufflike cuffs of soft gray fur, swirled and drifted about her. She flung out her arms and, smiling, rushed into her mother's embrace.

"Dana! My baby! We didn't hear you come—"

"Mother! Dad!" Dana's voice was low, with a throbbing, husky note in it. She moved from one to the other, lifting white arms, to kiss them on both cheeks. Her diaphanous wrap fell back to float round her like a mist on a light breeze. "But this is a lovely way to find you. And Dock!"

Her brother swung her up in his arms to kiss her soundly on the mouth. "None of that French stuff for me, my girl. I knew you when, you know." He turned to set her down on her feet before his wife.

"And little Daphne." Dana took Daphne's cool face between her palms, kissed her lightly on the forehead. "So sweet to find you here."

She turned gracefully, her amethyst eyes wide with anticipation. "And now—my babies! Where are they?"

Her voice was deeply emotional, tender. In the soft light she made a lovely picture. The dark, keen eyes of the man watching from the living room twinkled appreciatively.

"Where they should be," Dock told her callously. "In bed. Doctor's orders."

"In bed? They are ill!" The husky voice trembled. "My babies—"

"We didn't know when you'd get here," her mother explained mildly. "It seemed a pity to keep them up—for just a few minutes. They'd be sleepy tonight. Cross tomorrow."

"But to see their mummy!" She turned with a dramatic sweep toward the doors. "They are here?"

"They're at Mother's—where they've been for the past two years," Dock informed her. "And they know nothing yet about your return. Mother'll tell them in the morning. Send them over with Mademoiselle whenever you're ready for the great reunion. Now calm down, Sis, and produce the new husband."

"I can produce myself, young man," a deep voice rumbled. "Just thought I'd wait till the family greetings were over."

They turned from Dana as a short, compact man stepped out on the terrace. Though in the dim light his square shoulders and short legs made him appear shorter still, there was a bigness about him. Some vital force or electricity generated within him impressed and attracted them irresistibly. Not young, not old, he moved with the surety and authority of a man who knew where he was going, What he was doing every moment.

"Carter darling!" Dana flowed toward him, took his arm, led him to her parents. "You're family too. For always."

He did not speak as he took Mother Madison's hand, then Dad's. He looked up at each and straight into their eyes for a long moment. Then he turned to Daphne and Dock.

"I thought so," was his surprising comment. "Good stock, all of you. Character. Stability. Integrity. We'll get along. Orchids don't grow on bushes."

"Orchids?" Mother Madison repeated uncertainly.

He waited till she was seated, then drew up a wide chair beside her and Dad.

"Your daughter and my wife," he explained. "The orchid, Mrs. Madison, is a much-maligned flower. It is not a parasite. It does not live on others. But it requires something—something strong—a tree, or rock, or good soil, to support it while it lives an independent life of its own. That's our Dana."

Mother Madison smiled, still uncertain, but Dad and Dock laughed with him.

"Darling," Dana, cried tragically, "my babies—they aren't here—"

Coyne drew her down on the seat beside him. "One thing at a time, trinket. You've lived without them—not unhappily—for two years. A few more hours won't age them—or you. *Paciencia*. Ah!" he exclaimed as Chang appeared with whisky, glasses, and ice on a tray. "My favorite cure for snakebite."

The Chinese stopped, then quietly set down the tray on the table before Daphne and returned to the house. Silence froze the others in their chairs.

Instantly aware of the changed atmosphere, Coyne looked around. His glance sharpened. He fixed his eyes on Dock.

"Out with it, young man. I thought I'd simply used an old camp phrase out of turn. But I've done more than that, I see. What's on the collective mind?"

Dock's lips moved stiffly. "You don't know? Dana didn't tell you?"

"Evidently not." Coyne's gaze did not leave Dock's face, but his smallish, firm hand went out and gripped Dana's clenched ones reassuringly. She did not speak or move. Both his glance and his voice sharpened.

"I'm waiting for an explanation from someone."

"Dana should have told you," Dock said levelly. "But perhaps she couldn't. You'll understand why. You know she has been married before?"

"Yes. Twice. What's that got to do with it?"

"You know how her husbands died?"

"No."

"Of snakebite. Rattlesnake. Here."

"Go on."

"There isn't much danger—if one uses his head. But they're in the woods—that is, in some parts. Rattlers. Copperheads too. Fretz Dreier was an entomologist. He knew they were there. And he'd been all through the woods, chasing his crazy bugs and butterflies. But one day he was careless."

"I know. I've had men like that in my camps. And the other?"

"Blake Amery grew up in this valley—but on the other side—several miles from here. In a region of manicured estates where the 'No Trespassing' signs apply to snakes and bugs as well as to all but a handful of the human race. We live on what was called, when Dana and I were small fry, 'the back road.' Because Dad's farms and the old Hedley farm across the road were real dirt farms—and an eyesore to the country gentlemen—"

An infectious chuckle from Coyne interrupted him, drove the sardonic note from his voice as he went on.

"Life at Amery Chimneys and in New York hadn't prepared Blake Amery for life on Madison Farms. And he wasn't an easy man to tell what to do or not to do. One day he wandered into the woods. Why, God only knows.

Got lost. Days later Bixby—Dana's superintendent here—found him. Dead. Rattlesnake bite."

"Thank you," Coyne turned to Dana. "It's all right, my dear. Now I know. And you all know I know. I'm sorry I put my foot in my mouth the first time I opened it, but it's better to have these things clear—"

He stopped, sat perfectly still, his hand firm on his wife's. Dana was leaning back in the chair, her eyes closed, long lashes making dark pools of shadow on her cheeks. She had not moved, but under his hand he had felt her whole body grow taut, felt her intense concentration.

"Toy," he said gently, "don't feel badly. You weren't to blame. It's all in the past. We'll go on from here."

She flung his hand from hers, sprang to her feet. She wasn't acting now. For a moment she stood tense; listening, her face turned toward the road. Then, as if something pursued her, she fled across the terrace and vanished into the house.

Coyne rose, listening, too. So were the others. Faintly across the lawns came the strains of a violin.

5

Monday Morning, July 28

Mother Madison stood on the Madison veranda step, watching with misted eyes two reluctant little figures grow smaller slowly down the vista of Phlox Walk. Bunny in a scrap of blue pants, clinging to Whiffles' left hand. Whiffles, his thin body narrow as a blade in overalls, scuffling thoughtful feet through the soft grass. In his right hand he held preciously a battered shoe box.

This time they appeared to be definitely on their way. But twice they had returned. Once for Bunny to be assured she could come back as often as she wished. Once for Whiffles to ask if his room could be left as it was for a little while. From his back pocket now waved the impressive document Dad had given him, deeding the room to him forever and ever.

The requests, however, as Dad and Mother Madison understood too well, were surface anxieties cloaking another still deeper and closer to the youngsters' hearts. Mademoiselle. Sensitive to the stillness in her face and the emotional tumult of which she gave no outward sign, they had hovered like protecting birds about her all morning as she packed the last things for them. Now, uncertain of what lay ahead, they had tried to reassure themselves that the way was still open for them and their governess to return to the life they knew and loved.

As Mother Madison watched, Whiffles stopped as alertly as a bird dog. For a moment he looked across the phlox on his right to the fence enclosing the kitchen gardens, where his erratic, not to say erotic, gourd vines clambered.

"Jim!" she heard a now-familiar rumble calling. "What are these extraordinary gourds?"

She watched Whiffles set down his box carefully, disappear among the phlox. Within two breaths Bunny was following. After some time both reappeared, flanking Carter Coyne, and excitedly intent on something he was telling them.

Slowly all three went on up the walk, Bunny with a confiding hand in Coyne's, Whiffles walking sidewise to miss no word. Both children were so absorbed they forgot to turn to make sure she was still watching.

"I—I guess it's going to be all right," she said tremulously to Dad, watching her from the swing. "Carter came to meet them. They seem to—to like him."

Her husband swung thoughtfully for a minute. "I think Dana's come to land at last, Mother. C. C.'s a fine man—a good man. What I can't understand is—" He paused, concluded, "It's going to seem strange round here now—without the youngsters."

"Oh, they'll be running in and out." Mother Madison sat down heavily in a chair near him. "Funny that Whiffles wanted to go over alone, wasn't it?"

"He's a deep one. And he remembers. Bunny doesn't. This is the first time for her. Poor little Whiffles! Wanting a permanent place he could call his own—"

"And Mademoiselle's," she finished for him.

Dad sighed. "Let's not cross that bridge until we come to it."

Automatically Mother Madison repressed her own sigh, then smiled with affectionate understanding at her husband. She had heard that phrase so many times in their forty years of married life. Dad never crossed bridges, much less burned them behind him. Perhaps if he had, if he had not preferred the long way round always, Dana would not now own Madison Farms. And they would not now be living there practically as guests on the rent she paid them to maintain their ten acres in harmony with her own.

Dana was the bridge crosser of the family, she thought. Dana, not only crossed and burned bridges but built them for herself and others. Well, perhaps, as Dad had said, their daughter had come to land at last. Carter Coyne was a fine man, though she could understand no better than Dad why such a man should marry Dana.

"Here's C. C. now," Dad said, sitting up.

She turned. Carter Coyne was strolling toward them across the lawn from Phlox Walk as if he'd lived on Madison Farms for years. His head was bare. In an old shirt, open at the throat, worn twill riding trousers, high-laced boots, he obviously felt at home with himself and the entire place.

When he saw them looking at him he waved an informal salute. "Hi!"

A moment more and he was beside them on the veranda, nodding at Mother Madison, beaming on Dad like an old crony. "Should be good fishing around here somewhere," he suggested. "I saw a river on the other side of the woods just now."

Dad's face warmed with pleasure, grew sad.

"I know," Coyne said quickly. "Bad heart; that's it, isn't it, Dad? But couldn't you sit as quietly in a boat as in that swing? I'm about to burst with dammed-up energy. I'll do the rowing, lifting, for both of us. Cussing too."

Dad's face brightened again. "Brother, I'm your man. When do we start?"

"You're the captain, sir. When you give the word. Right now I've come to have a little chat with you and Mother

Madison." He paused before seating himself to wave a hand toward Phlox Walk. "Met the offspring just now. Fine pair, aren't they? We'll get along."

"You came to meet them," Mother Madison accused, smiling.

"Well, our meeting wasn't all accident. Thought I'd like to see them first on their own ground—and mine. Children—American children—are pretty realistic. So am I. Thought if Dana didn't have an audience for their reunion she might be more—less—oh, you know—" He waved a hand to finish the thought for him.

"Is it the children you want to talk about?" Mother Madison prompted.

He shook his head. "No. About Dana, myself, you, all of us. Rather like locking the barn door after the horse is stolen, though, isn't it, to talk to you now when Dana and I are married?"

"And not necessary unless you want to yourself," Dad assured him. "We—Mother and I—are satisfied. Perfectly."

"Include me too." Coyne smiled and with a nod indicated the grounds. "This is just the sort of place I've wanted all my life. You're the sort of people. I guess finding you here is a kind of reward for all the hard years."

He drew his chair forward to face them more squarely. "I came because I thought you'd like to know why a man like me and a woman like Dana should—or could—come together. She's twenty-eight. I'm twice that. It wasn't love, of course. You must have seen that. But each of us had what the other wanted. Funny. Neither of us placed any value on what we had ourselves. Though I guess that's not peculiar to Dana and me."

Coyne shrugged. "Dana wanted money. Not for itself or for herself, really. For something she wants to do with it. She must have been hurt pretty badly once—for lack of it."

His voice rose slightly, could have signaled a question if they had cared to answer it. When they said nothing he went on.

"Well, I have money. That is, I assume I have. Don't know what this war's going to do to it, of course. Taxes and what not. But that's all right with me. The government could have it all if it weren't for Dana. I want her to realize some dream she's got in her mind about this place—you people."

He shrugged that away too. "The point is, she gets what she wants married to me. I get what I want married to her."

He turned his massive, good-boned head to look out over the grounds to Dana's home. "Something young and full of life and lovely. At first I took her at face value—as an amusing and pretty trinket. An orchid, as I said last night."

Turning back, he smiled at Mother Madison. "I've never had much real pleasure or fun—getting my money. Working in camps. Out West. In China, Russia, South America. Learning how the world wags the hard way. When I got it there were plenty of ways to spend it, of course. But I was too old for them. And I'd seen too many men near the 'crazy sixties' play the fool with wealth—

"Then I met Dana. Saw her, rather. In Buenos Aires first. Gambling in the casinos. I got more fun than I think I'd ever had up to that time just watching her spend what she had. It wasn't a little, but it wasn't enough, either. Because she isn't a born gambler. She finds no pleasure in it. She plays to win and takes fearful risks. Sometimes she wins; sometimes she doesn't. But win or lose, she never falters, turns back. To see that little triangular face of hers set, those incredible eyes of hers turn purple—"

Coyne chuckled aloud in delighted memory. "I can see that doesn't amuse you, but it did me. Though she had no idea how funny she was, of course."

Dad's eyes twinkled in understanding, but Mother Madison's face was grave with disapproval.

"I found out she was flying round South America," Coyne resumed after a moment. "And I made it my business to be where she was. Partly because I got such a kick out of watching her. Partly because I thought she needed someone round—just in case."

He chuckled again, deep in his throat. "I needn't have worried. Dana's perfectly capable of taking care of Dana wherever she is. In Bogota, where I'm known and she could find out all about me if she wanted to, I asked her to marry me. You know perhaps how they've been trying to consolidate the tin mines down there to speed up war production. Well, I sold out and checked out. I've plenty of things to keep me busy in this country. And here we are."

He fell silent, though obviously he had not finished what he had to say. Mother Madison and Dad remained comfortably silent, too, waiting.

"I'd seen plenty of young women like Dana," Coyne resumed after a moment. "Gay and pretty opportunists, I'd found them, in all parts of the world. Featherbrained, too, I'd thought them, until I saw Dana. She was no featherweight. I knew there was good blood behind her, also—the way she saw things through to the end. But—well, I guess my life's made me hard, overcareful. I made one condition before we were married.

"My money is hers—all of it—and more if she needs me to get more—as long as she remains my wife. I've made a name for myself. A good one. Respected. I intend to keep it that way. I promised her if the day ever came when she met a younger man—someone she really wanted to marry—I'd free her. Make a generous settlement, step out of the picture. She'd only need to tell me."

Abruptly Coyne stood up, facing them in a wide, firm stance. "But I warned her then that if she ever met such a man and didn't tell me—tried to eat her cake and have it—I'd ruin her and the man too."

Swinging away from their now-grave faces, he paced the veranda, came back.

"I'm telling you this for two reasons. One, because I planned to tell you before we came—so there'd be no misunderstanding later. And second, because now I'm here I—I want to stay. As I said, this is the kind of place and life I've dreamed—in jungles and mining camps—I'd like one day. And I'm the kind of man to fight to get and to keep what I want."

His deep voice, the emphasis he gave to the last sentence lifted Dad's and Mother Madison's eyes in startled question.

"I've always found it smart business to follow my hunches," he went on slowly. "And I've a hunch now there's a man behind that violin playing last night. Someone who matters to Dana."

6

Monday Morning, July 28

He studied their quickly veiled faces. "So—I was right. I knew Dreier and Amery didn't count. Last night my hand was on Dana's when that violin began to play. She didn't move, but I felt some shock run through her. I knew it wasn't what Dock had said that caused it."

Again he took a step or two up and down the veranda. He seemed to be formulating, discarding sentences that half moved his lips.

"Look here," he said abruptly, coming back to them. "This fiddle scraper. I hadn't anticipated anything like this—an old sweetheart on the doorstep. But perhaps it could be worse. I know Dana. My name had as much to do with her marrying me as my money. An unknown—and probably poverty-ridden—country fiddler doesn't bother me. And he should be easy to dispose of. Think you could buy him out for me, Dad, get rid of him?"

Dad looked at Mother Madison, slowly shook his head.

"No? Well, perhaps you're right. An old friend, all that. But there's no reason why I shouldn't make him an offer myself, is there? If he wants to farm he can find better land than this all over the country. If he wants to fiddle, the money should make it possible for him to get somewhere with it—"

Coyne stopped, his eyes sharp on the conflict of expressions his listeners' faces were recording.

"You don't understand, Carter," Mother Madison said reluctantly. "He—he's Hedrick."

"Hedrick?" For a moment the name obviously meant nothing to Coyne. Then he recognized it. "Hedrick! You don't mean the Norwegian—"

Mother Madison nodded. "*The* Hedrick."

Coyne sat down, still unbelieving. "Let's get this straight," he said finally. "Dana loves or loved this man? Then why hasn't she married him? What was she doing playing around South America?"

"She doesn't know," Mother Madison explained unhappily. "I mean, she doesn't know he's Hedrick now. He's been in Europe for years. None of us knew—until he came back a year ago."

"By us, Mother means just Dock and Daphne, she and I know he's Rick Hedley," Dad interrupted. "To everyone else he's Hedrick. Living on the old Hedley farm."

"Go on."

Dad went on reluctantly: "His real name's Richard Hedley, but from the day he was born he's been Rick to us. His father farmed that land across the road. Hed, we called him. Hedleys have owned that land as long as the Madisons this. For generations. Hed was a strange fellow. Always going off in the winters to travel, anything to spend the money he made in the fall off his fields. Mother and I were married about five years, I guess, when he came back one spring married to a Norwegian girl—"

"Helga Gislason," Mother supplied.

"Hed traveled no more after that. Settled down to real farming when Rick was born. Helga was a wonderful woman, helped him a lot. Had a beautiful singing voice. Remember, Mother? And she played the violin. Was teaching Rick almost as soon as he could stand. She died when he was ten years old, but by that time she'd made him a fiddler. He had no interest in the farm.

"Hed hadn't much, either, after her death. But he stayed on, making a home for his fiddle-playing son. When he died, about nine, ten years ago, we didn't know what would become of Rick, but he solved the situation for himself. Took what little money there was and went to his mother's people in Norway."

Coyne was not deceived by Dad's casual tone. "Took what little there was of whose money?" he asked shrewdly.

Dad and Mother Madison exchanged glances. Dad nodded. "Mine, I guess," he admitted but said no more.

Coyne had listened patiently, but now he turned his eyes in compelling question on Mother Madison. "And Dana?" he asked.

"There's no reason why you shouldn't know," she told him. "When I tell you you'll see how perfectly natural it all was. Dad and I had been married about two years when Dock was born. He was four when Rick was born. The only children around here, they were playing together as soon as Rick could toddle. Dad and I wanted a daughter very much, so when Dock was five we adopted Daphne."

She paused to smile reminiscently at her husband. "Dock abandoned Rick for his new sister. When Dana arrived, three years later, he simply wasn't interested in her. Daphne was his whole world, as she is now. So Rick took care of Dana from the time she was a baby. In fact, he considered her his personal property, just as Dock thought of Daphne. 'My Dana,' Rick called her. It was funny to see the four of them together then."

"That's the way it was, C. C.," Dad said, nodding. "But it stopped being funny, as Mother calls it, when Dock and Daphne married, and we thought Rick and Dana were going to follow their example. Not that there was anything against Rick except that he was no farmer, and it never occurred to us, of course, that he'd ever be able to do anything playing that fiddle.

"Mother worried a good deal, but I didn't—until—well, something happened we don't need to mention here. With the fantastic ideas Dana had about money—and other things— I never thought she'd marry a poor man. My fault, I guess, her ideas. I—I had them, too—only mine never came to anything."

His voice grew thinner as he talked, stopped.

"Something happened to change Dana's mind?" Coyne prompted.

"Well, yes," Dad admitted reluctantly. "They loved one another—no question about that. I—I guess they'd have married if it hadn't been for Rick's fiddle. Dana wouldn't marry a fiddler, and Rick wouldn't—couldn't, maybe—give it up. One night Dana went so far as to throw it in the fire. That was when, to save them both, I offered him what I had to go to Europe to study."

"A choice between Dana and his fiddle?" Coyne asked dryly.

"No choice, really. The boy couldn't live without that violin. He left the next morning for New York. Then Norway. Dana's never seen him since."

Mother Madison inserted, "Dad managed the farm, took care of everything, until Rick returned a year ago."

"And Dana?" Coyne prompted again.

"She began to change then. Hard to say just how. She never mentioned Rick's name again. Never said much about anything. Finally, to help her forget him, forget a lot of things, we sent her to Cornell. In her second year she came back, just at Christmas, married to Fretz Dreier, an exchange professor there, from Holland."

"A fine man," Mother Madison inserted again, "but not at all the husband for Dana."

"All wrapped up in his work," Dad explained. "Turned this whole place into a laboratory. Knew every bug and butterfly for miles around by its first name. Sort of considered Dana, too, as a rare species of butterfly. Left her plenty of time to think about Rick."

Mother Madison sighed. "We thought when Whiffles was born she'd forget, settle down. But she didn't. Perhaps she would have if Fretz had lived."

Coyne's head stopped pendulating from one to the other. "But when and how did this Rick become Hedrick? And why doesn't she know?" he demanded.

"He never wrote." Dad stirred uncomfortably. "It was just as if he had stepped off into space. All we knew was that he'd gone to Europe, probably Norway. About four, five years ago, we know now, someone discovered him. Suddenly he became a sensation all over Europe. But Rick Hedley was still a fiddler to us, and if we ever heard his new name we never associated it with our Rick. Never knew till he came back and American papers began raving about him that our Rick Hedley was now the great Hedrick."

Coyne ground his palms together, tapped them thoughtfully between his knees on the seat of his chair. "Any ideas about what to do?"

Dad looked at his wife, troubled, shook his head. "Perhaps it isn't necessary to do anything," he suggested. "Dana may never see Rick. He doesn't leave his own place except to go into New York. I believe he can't."

"Can't?"

"Something about his contracts or agents. They didn't want him to come out here at all. Don't want it known he's American. I believe they feel that as a Norwegian violinist—"

Coyne laughed. "He'll make more money for them. I know."

"He won't come to see us. We don't go there—any more. And in a few weeks he leaves anyway—to play for the Army camps before he goes on his own concert tour."

"You think Dana may never see him?" Coyne was skeptical, then jumped to his feet, "When you don't know what to do, do nothing. The next move's up to Dana. Let's go look over the fishing possibilities, Dad."

He turned as the screen doors opened and the governess stepped out on the veranda. His eyes missed nothing of her tall, well-proportioned figure, her poise and breeding. But they centered on the smooth oval of her face, from which black hair was drawn back severely into braids laced across the back of her head. This severity and lack of make-up emphasized eyes so dark and shining, so limpid that they appeared liquid, and the full, soft lips she was obviously making a determined effort to control.

When Mother Madison introduced her as Mademoiselle he took her hand with a friendly smile but did not speak. Neither did she. And she turned quickly to say, "Everything is ready now, Mrs. Madison."

Coyne's eyes concentrated again, partly because he recognized her low, throaty voice as the model for Dana's, partly because every tone and movement revealed that Mademoiselle was no ordinary governess.

"Run along then," Mother Madison said, smiling. "Pete will carry the bags over when he comes in for lunch." She took Mademoiselle's hand, held it firmly until the tremulous lips steadied. "Remember, we aren't losing you, my dear. Dad and I expect you and the children every day—"

"Thank you, madame." The governess turned to Dad.

"Of course we aren't losing you," he assured her. "And personally I'm borrowing you back whenever Mother's Russian bank takes a turn for the worse."

"Thank you." Mademoiselle plainly could not trust herself to say more. She smiled with her lips at Coyne and walked quickly to the side step of the veranda.

There she paused, as if reluctant to go farther. Her head turned to the left, and she looked for a long minute at the wing of the house banked with green shrubbery. Then resolutely she stepped down and walked across the lawn to Phlox Walk.

"Good God!" Coyne exclaimed when she was out of earshot. "What's the matter with the woman? And how long has she been in charge of the small fry?"

"Since shortly after Whiffles was born," Dad told him. "Fretz got her for Dana. She's Belgian,"

As if in answer to some unspoken criticism he felt in Coyne, he added, "And she's a wonder. Couldn't care for the children or love them more if she were their mother. And she's a wonderful teacher too. Wait till you hear Whiffles' French. Even Bunny's."

"Rather an emotional type, isn't she?" Coyne asked. He looked after the tall figure, now far down Phlox Walk, shrugged. "Well, let's go, Dad."

Mother Madison watched them go. Dad, tall and frail, moved slowly. Coyne walked slowly, too, but something of the vitality he could not suppress, something in the square set of his head and shoulders troubled her. He looked to be what he had said he was—a man who would fight to get and to keep what he wanted.

Suddenly she saw she was not the only one watching the two ill-matched figures moving toward the path that led through the orchards to the woods. Branches of lilac hedge concealing the kitchen gardens from the house thrust aside briefly. Bixby's dark head peered out, withdrew.

As she turned back to the house she saw the superintendent emerge on Phlox Walk, stride rapidly down it toward Dana's home.

7
Monday Noon, July 28

Sitting on the floor of her sitting room, a soundlessly thrilled Bunny on one side, a loudly excited Whiffles on the other, Dana, happy, though slightly worn, was annoyed to hear the little Swiss bell on her door tinkle softly.

By the exertion of every charm she possessed she had managed in something more than an hour to gain a finger-hold on her children's affection and allegiance. Interruption at this point by anyone—even to herself she would not admit that by anyone she meant Mademoiselle—was unwelcome.

She looked from one to the other of the intent youngsters, deep in gifts and bright wrapping papers. They had not even heard the bell. Relieved, she called, "Come in."

Ellen, one of the new maids, entered. "A man—he says his name is Bixby—is here to see you, Mrs. Coyne."

Dana half rose, sank back. "Bixby is my superintendent, Ellen." With a smile she indicated the children. "Tell him I cannot see him now. Later, perhaps."

A shriek of delight from Bunny dismissed Bixby and the maid from her mind. The little girl was holding high a Peruvian man doll, carved from wood.

"You like it, precious? Look again. Somewhere you'll find a little wife for him."

She turned to the deeply silent Whiffles. He had opened but one of his gifts, an enormous box, overflowing with tracks, switches, bridges, all the amazing equipment of an electric train system. Parts of it were strewn around him. Most of it still remained in its box. Now after an outburst of wild excitement when he saw it he sat looking soberly at the mound of still-unwrapped packages beside him.

"Don't you like the train, darling? Daddy Carter brought it to you. You're going to like him too?"

Whiffles nodded vigorously. "He calls me Jim. He—he said to call him Carter—just Carter." Shy pleasure shone in his clear eyes, a little fear, too, that she might not approve.

"Jim? But of course. That's your real name, isn't it?" Her face matched his in earnestness. "Naturally when you men are together it should be Jim and Carter."

She gave his shoulders an affectionate shake. "But that doesn't mean I'm to lose my Whiffles, does it? Now, let's open the rest of your things."

He freed himself to look at her soberly again. "But I—I have only one present for you," he said wistfully. "And Bunny has none. She's too young. And I—I haven't any for Carter—"

Again the Swiss bell tinkled. This time Ellen brought a square of blue paper. Dana took it impatiently, motioned her to leave.

Just a weekly report of Bixby's, she thought, glancing at it. But when she started to toss it aside a line written in soft pencil across the bottom caught her eye. As she read her eyes darkened.

"Five o'clock, p and m. Sure. Bixby." The "sure" was heavily underscored.

Whiffles, watching, drew closer. "What is it, Mummy?"

She drove the quick anger from her voice and face. "Nothing. Nothing at all, angel."

Tearing off the scribbled line, she crumpled the bit of paper in her hand, then impatiently tossed both pieces aside.

"Let's get on with the presents, shall we? It's almost time for your luncheon. What are you looking for, Whiffles?"

He had jumped up as she spoke to look anxiously about the room. Now he was burrowing into the mound of papers Bunny had flung about. He came up, smiling, with his battered shoe box in both hands. Carefully he carried it to her.

"It's my present. Maybe—if you count each one—a lot of presents." His eyes turned to the pile of unopened gifts she had brought him.

Dana swept a space clear before her, received the box from him as carefully. "My first present from my son. Darling! I can't wait to see it."

Pleased, he dropped on his knees beside her, lifted the lid.

She gasped, then caught him close to hide for a moment her surprise and distaste.

"It's—they're wonderful!" she assured the top of his head with all the enthusiasm she could muster. "And such a lot of presents. Many more than we brought you."

Whiffles rewarded her with a shining glance before he bent to look himself at the motley collection of beetles the box contained.

"They're pretty good, aren't they? I—I worked awful hard to get them. And Mam'selle helped me to fix them." Manfully he kept his eyes from the gifts he now felt free to open.

A little shaken by the gift and his pride in it, Dana capitulated completely. "Do you know what? I think some of your father's cases—specimen cases—are still around somewhere. If not, we'll get one—a big one. And right after luncheon you're to choose the one place in the house you'd like to hang your—my—our collection."

"Gee!" Whiffles wriggled with pleasure. To hide it, he seized the nearest package.

Cluckings on her left drew Dana's attention hurriedly. But Bunny was really happy. She had found the wife of the Peruvian doll and was exploring its costume with chubby fingers. As Dana watched they found a tiny pocket in the black wool skirt. But the pocket, alas, was empty.

Quick concern puckered the intense little face. Bunny glanced about, spied the crumpled bit of blue paper Dana had tossed away. Before Dana could suggest a substitute, she had tucked it in the pocket. Content then, she sat back, crooning and rocking the doll in her arms.

Restraining her impulse to recover that insolent message, Dana sat back between the two youngsters. Before her delight in this silent intimacy with her children, her indignation at Bixby melted. She looked about the large, luxurious room, bright with summer sunshine pouring in through opened windows and French doors, enjoying the sense of possession and stability it gave her.

In less than ten years she had won all this. Won it herself, by her own efforts. Now she was safe, secure, bulwarked forever. She could begin to build the life she wanted for herself, the children, the whole family.

Almost unbelievingly she realized it. Realized, too, how tired she was now that it was all over, that she could lean back.

The tinkle of the Swiss bell recalled her. Mademoiselle entered. Before Dana could move the children were on their feet, clamoring for the governess's attention to their gifts. Smiling, Mademoiselle spoke to them softly in French. After a moment they freed her hands but did not return to Dana.

"Welcome home, madame." The governess's half-lifted hand fell to her side when Dana, annoyed, did not offer hers.

"Oh, hello, Mademoiselle. How are you?" Dana smiled up from the floor, waved expressively toward the chaos about her. "We're home again, you see."

"Yes, madame. I'm sure the children are—very happy."

"You've been up to their floor? Everything is in order?"

"Certainly, madame. I arranged everything Saturday. The last things will come over today."

"Excellent. Will you unpack for me, then, this afternoon? And see that all this"—Dana waved her hands toward the gifts—"is taken upstairs? You've come for the children now?"

"Their luncheon is ready." Mademoiselle spoke to the children again in French. They raced from the room, Bunny stopping to secure the Peruvian doll wife.

"Mrs. Madison has just telephoned," Mademoiselle said then to Dana. "Mr. Coyne and her husband have gone off to the river, she says. She'd like you to have luncheon with her."

Quick decision flashed in Dana's eyes. "Tell her I'll come as soon as I've made one telephone call. Get Bixby for me, will you, on my phone?"

The governess hesitated, then moved to the low table near the French doors and lifted the receiver from its cradle. Dana paid little attention to the call. Her eyes were fixed on Mademoiselle in cool appraisal.

Mademoiselle caught that glance as she replaced the receiver. Bixby wasn't home, she said. His daughter Mary didn't expect him back until after his five-o'clock appointment with Mrs. Coyne.

8

Monday Afternoon, July 28

Her face closed with anger, Dana returned home in the late afternoon to change into slacks and stout shoes. What had happened to Bixby during these past two years? she wondered repeatedly as she dressed. Her mother had left nothing unsaid concerning the superintendent's deliberate neglect of the Farms. Concerning his relentless pursuit of Mademoiselle.

And she who once would have listened to no criticism, even from her mother, of anything or anyone that came under the head of her possessions had been unable to reply. Because of the rankling memory of that scribbled message in pencil Bixby had sent her.

She wouldn't be silent long, she promised herself as she hurried from her room into the long corridor that ran through the house. She'd get to the bottom of this—and probably find Mademoiselle! This was not the first time the governess, with her doelike eyes and seductive ways, had caused trouble. But it would certainly be the last.

Resentment, suspicion gave bite to her voice when she met Mademoiselle on the east terrace. "Tell the children I've gone for a walk, will you? I'll be back before their supper."

"You are going into the woods—to the pools, perhaps, madame?" At Dana's sharp glance the governess added quickly, "Then you must take a stick. The paths are not good, and sometimes it is necessary to jump. One moment. I will bring you mine."

She disappeared within the house. Dana waited impatiently, disturbed again by that stillness in the woman's manner.

The governess returned, a sturdy cane in her hand. "This is strong, madame. I have used it in Switzerland for climbing."

Danas fingers clasped easily about its unusual head, a metal reproduction of a ram's horn, fitted solidly into oak. "Thanks, Mademoiselle. I shan't be long."

Idly swinging the stick, she circled the house to steps leading down the back terrace to the driveway. Across it she reached a path that wound through apple orchards to the north woods. In her absorption she hardly noticed the trees on either side, their branches arched beneath the weight of young apples.

The path ended at an opening in a low stone wall that served as the entrance to picnic grounds. She merely glanced at the huge stone fireplace, the benches and tables arranged beneath spreading maples. Cutting across the soft grass to the right, she entered a narrow road. There she stopped for the first time, her eyes narrowing with anger.

Only partially cleared of roots and underbrush, it wound through dense woods. Holes, stones, and rough chunks of cement scattered along it made it anything but the idyllic walk she had expected to find. Increasingly angry with each step, she picked a way, first on one side, then on the other. At length, as an opening in the trees showed ahead, she slowed her pace.

She came out on a mass of tumbled stones and blocks of old cement. It covered the ground for a distance of several yards to end abruptly at a slight rise and more woods. Incredulous, she stopped short again.

Here, with crowding trees shutting away all but a glimpse of the bright afternoon sky, the scene was desolate, almost dark. Two years before a charming little stream had rippled over a pebble bed as an outlet for two pools, Pelleas and Melisande, that had lain side by side on the right, joined by a narrow channel. Now the rocks and cement, assisted by outlaw masses of wild blackberry bushes and weeds, choked—in fact, effaced—all sign of the stream.

And what had once been two clear pools was now a slough of stagnant water hidden beneath a thick arsenical green scum. Branches of oaks and elms that once had mirrored themselves there now drooped disconsolately over it, adding to the sense of desolation. Even the humming of insects in the warm air and the plunk! plunk! of a single frog were now lugubrious sounds.

Slowly, using the stick to aid her on the tilting stones, gazing with cold fury at that dead green surface, Dana moved forward. A sound stopped her. Bixby, sitting on a pile of cement chunks, half hidden by blackberry branches, was rising lazily to his feet.

"What is the meaning of this?" she demanded without preamble.

"Meaning, Miss Dana?"

"Of your impudent note! Of your daughter's message! Now—this!"

"Well, now, Miss Dana, that's a funny tone to take after two years." He smiled slowly as he approached. "Meaning of the note is I thought we'd better have a little talk, first thing, you and me. And this is a good place. No one comes here any more."

As she continued to face him, inflexible with anger, he waved a careless hand toward the slough. "Meaning of this— Well, one reason for that rattlesnake pest we seemed to be having around here was that the pesky serpents used to follow the stream in here to the pools. I just dried it up for them. Now they have to stay in those rocks and high grass yonder or go back where they came from. That was the idear, wasn't it? To make the woods—safe?"

She turned from him furiously to look out over the dead water. "Look at that! Ruined! Worse than a swamp!"

"Would have cost a heap of money to do all you wanted, Miss Dana."

"What do you think I was paying you for these past two years? Mother says you've had four men just to keep the lawns and gardens in shape. That you haven't done a thing yourself."

He took a step toward her, unsmiling now, to tower over her. "Reckon I did what you paid me for, Miss Dana," he said slyly. "Kept my mouth shut."

Cunning moved in his eyes as she retreated before him. "Reckon I can keep on doing that, long as you pay me. Though now you're home, I thought we'd better—improve my terms."

Dana stiffened. She faced him now, anger blazing in her eyes and voice. "That's enough. Because of Mary I'm giving you twenty-four hours to pack up and leave."

Bixby smiled again. "We've grown mighty fond of life here, Miss Dana. Suits me, suits my girl."

"You heard me!" Turning her back, Dana started to return.

His rough square hand flashed out, seized her arm, swung her round. Too angry to speak now, she whipped herself free, half raised her stick.

"Listen, Mrs. Coyne," he said with calculated insolence. "You ain't telling me nothing from now on. I'm telling you. Oh, I guess Fretz Dreier died, right enough, of rattlesnake trouble. Anyway, I don't know no different. But no snake got Blake Amery."

Dana became completely still. Not even her eyes showed life.

"Not that I blame you much, I think, myself, a man who ain't fit to live with, no matter how much money he's got, ain't fit to live. But some folks don't think that way, Miss Dana. They'd be mighty interested to know how Blake Amery died. The old Senator, for one."

He stopped, mistrustful of her silence. She stood rigid before him, her face, in the greenish light, paper white, her eyes fixed on his in unbelieving horror.

"That's better. Now you know I know, I guess we can talk business. You wanted millions. Well—you've got them. Guess I helped you to get them, didn't I? Guess you'd like me to help you keep 'em—"

A smile moved in his eyes as she slowly lowered the stick. She tried to speak, but only a husky croak issued from her lips. He waited coolly. At last she forced her lips to serve her.

"How much do you want?"

"I've done a lot of thinking about that these two years," he began shrewdly. "Had to change all my idears, of course, when I heard you'd married this Carter Coyne. The way I see it now—you pay me by check one thousand dollars a month. If anyone wants to know I can say that's my salary plus ordinary expenses for keeping up this place."

He put up a hand hastily to prevent her speaking. "That ain't all, of course. I guess that little head of yours can figure out a way to get a hundred thousand to me on the side."

Her hand closed convulsively about the ram's head, raised the cane. With an easy swing of his arm he swept it aside. "None of that!" As she still held it raised he added mockingly, "You heard *me!*"

When she did not move or lower the cane he lunged forward to take it from her. She backed away from him, her face strained now with physical fear of him.

He stopped, laughed harshly, waved toward the unbroken green surface of the water below them. "Think I couldn't toss you in there as easy as a pebble? And nobody'd ever know. That pond's ten feet deep maybe now, but only two feet of it's clear water. Rest is mush, getting mushier."

She backed away again. "You're mad! Crazy! Keep away from me—"

Clumsily he tried to reassure her. "You're the crazy one! Think I'd hurt the little goose that's going to lay me golden eggs?"

Dana did not speak again. Out of a face white and icily cold her eyes were studying him with such concentration they appeared black. Slowly she drew in her breath, sucking in her lower lip. Two small white upper teeth appeared, biting into it.

Suspicion lighted in his face. He leaned forward, staring at her.

Under his gaze her body swayed. Her eyelids fluttered, half closed. The hand holding the cane opened nervelessly. With a clatter the stick fell to the stones at their feet.

Awkwardly he stooped to pick it up. But she was before him. Like a vise, her fingers closed on the heel of the cane, swung it high. Before he could straighten she brought the ram's horn down with all her strength on his head.

His knees sagged. He staggered but by brute strength managed to keep himself on his feet. Blindly, his arms stretched forward, he sought to seize her. For a breath Dana stood tense, watchful, out of his grasp, then raised the stick again. And again.

Still he did not fall. Still, though almost on his knees now, a horrible choking sound issuing from his throat, he sought her. Closer and closer she led him to the brink of the stones.

Rage, fear, horror, the basic instinct for self-preservation gave her power beyond her physical strength. She dropped the cane and flew at him, pushing him nearer the edge. He tried to turn, stumbled, slipped on a loose stone. Fell forward. Fell with a crash into the slough.

The thick green coating parted suddenly, shivering as it pushed back on all sides. A surface of lead-gray water showed, grew wider, then roiled as layer after layer of sediment surged up from the depths.

Motionless, Dana stood above it until the surface began to clear again. And the green scum, inch by inch, to close.

9

Monday Afternoon, July 28

In the stillness the crack of a dried stick reverberated like a rifleshot. Dana's head remained motionless, but her eyes moved swiftly to the right. No one was visible on the road by which she had come. No one could be behind her or on her left.

Nevertheless, when the crackle was repeated from the left, she turned her head. Then whirled round. Stood rigid.

A man stood there at the top of the slight rise, framed in the green of overhanging branches he was holding back. A tall, slender man, almost as blond as herself, clad in a worn open-throated shirt, faded blue shorts.

As she gazed at him he stepped down onto the stones, moved toward her. His eyes, deep-set in a lean, almost ascetic face, were fixed on hers.

"Rick!" she whispered incredulously.

"My Dana!"

He sprang toward her, caught her as she swayed—really swayed—dangerously near the brink of the slough. For a moment he supported her, then he drew her back to safer ground.

"I frightened you," he said gently, a hint of some foreign accent in his voice. "I should have spoken, called out first. But I couldn't believe—I didn't know you were home."

"You saw—" She was still gazing at him as if he were some fantasy of her mind. "You came—"

"Just now. Suddenly I saw you. Standing there—looking at the horrible thing you've made of our pools."

Her head was clearing. She freed herself, stood erect. Her eyes, traveling slowly from his head to his feet, registered every detail of his appearance, paused on his rounded, oddly stitched sandals.

"Rick!" she repeated, looking up at him again. "You're really Rick! Oh!" She shrank away from him. "Oh, why did you come?"

"Hush, my Dana. No wonder you're upset. Coming back—seeing all this—remembering. Then to have me appear! Sit down a moment. Here."

Half carrying her, he led her to the cement blocks beside the blackberry bushes. "Why did you come here alone? And at this hour? See, it already grows dark here."

She sank down limply, then, remembering, tried to rise. "Not here. Not now, Rick. I—I must go home." Vaguely she looked about.

"Your stick?"

He left her to pick it up from where it lay on the edge of the stone bank. For a moment he stood beside it, looking down at the jagged patch of open water in the mass of unbroken green. When he stooped he did not touch the cane. He filled his hands with small stones and bits of cement.

Lightly, idly, to give her time to recover from the shock of seeing him, he flicked one after the other over the pond. When the last stone was thrown the green surface was dotted with jagged patches of open water.

Then he picked up the cane, examined with interest its unusual head. Before he turned back to her he took out his handkerchief and wiped the stick carefully from head to heel.

"Ready?" he asked then.

Dana rose unsteadily. He hastened to her and took her arm. "Shall we go back my way? I come here so often I've worn a very good path. It brings you out on the road just above Dock's. You can go home from there through the grounds or down the road to your main entrance."

Talking quietly, he helped her over the stones and up the rise to a narrow, winding path. "I'll go ahead," he said there. "Warn you of the bad spots. Be careful. It's slippery at times."

He stepped in front of her, swinging the cane by the heel to lop off with the ram's horn tips of outjutting bushes, to thrust aside pebbles, fragments of branches, green balls of hickory nuts.

Dana followed silently, blindly, until they reached a tiny clearing. Like a small, vaulted chapel, enclosed on all sides by trees but free of underbrush, it was a welcome sight after the gloom of the slough.

Sunlight still penetrated here, lay warm on the remains of an aged stone wall that marked the limits of the original Madison farm. The wall had been cleared of vines and shrubs for a short space and, with other stones placed before it, formed a wide, low seat. Beyond it the land dropped sharply to a narrow valley where, through breaks in the tiered green of the woods, a silvery river shone luminously.

"Remember?" Rick turned to smile at her. She looked at the seat, turned quickly away.

"And see—our old path's still here." He parted some branches on her left, his lips twisting wryly. "You see I know about everything—except you. It now ends in your picnic grounds. Shall I take you back this way?"

She shook her head. "Let me go alone, Rick. Please. I know the way. I—I don't want our meeting to be—like this—"

"My Dana! Sweet, look at me." He grasped her arms, forcing her to lift her eyes. "I'm Rick. Your Rick. Don't I know what you're feeling? Don't I feel too?"

"Tomorrow," she murmured. "Tomorrow. Here. I'll come back. Let me go now."

He drew her closer. "You have come back, my Dana. Dana, Dana—"

She stood enclosed in his arms but remote, withdrawn. At last he released her, stepped back. "Tomorrow, then."

He watched her enter the vague path, disappear shortly among the massed trees. For a time he listened, following her progress with intent ears. When sounds died away he remained thoughtful, looking about the little clearing.

Dana's stick lay at his feet. He had no memory of dropping it. Now he hesitated before picking it up.

With sudden savagery he seized it by the heel, swung the head again and again upon the rough stones of the wall. Then swiftly he took a few steps down the path she had gone, dropped it to the ground.

In the clearing once more, he did not pause or continue to follow the path to the road and his home. With grim face he hurried back the way they had come to the pond.

10

Monday Afternoon, July 28

Dana did not pause either until she reached the picnic grounds. As she stepped free of the trees she stopped, startled. The sun was bright here on the soft green grass, made brighter still by wild yellow daisies and shafts of diffused sunlight pouring through branches of maple and birch.

Slowly she crossed the quiet grounds to a bench, sank down on it gratefully. Her knees, her hands, her whole body shook then as if freezing with cold.

There she remained in complete and studied stillness until the warmth and quiet of the scene warmed and quieted her. She looked about. Sat up, purposeful now.

Not yet six, her wrist watch told her. Not yet an hour since she had accepted that cane from Mademoiselle, set off for the appointment at Pelleas and Melisande.

For the first time she missed the stick. Looked about. Remembered it swinging from Rick's hand.

Rick! She half rose, then sank back. She mustn't think of Rick now. Or of the stick. Tomorrow . . .

Deliberately, with steady fingers, she took a compact from the pocket of her shirt, snapped open the mirror. The slender face that looked back at her was pale. The eyes shadowed, stiff, drugged with emotion.

She massaged them gently, her face, her throat. When she looked again faint color showed. She gazed into the little mirror until she could force both her lips and eyes to smile. Only then did she allow herself to think back—and ahead.

Rigorously she went over every moment of the day. Every word she had said, every action. To no one had she mentioned Bixby's message, her intention of seeing him. No one would question the fact that she had gone for a walk—she walked an hour every day when she was home. No one would think it strange she had gone first of all to the pools. If she had not, that would have appeared strange.

No one would question her word if she declared she had not seen Bixby. He had been too clever. He had kept out of sight all afternoon, to avoid meeting her openly, in the presence of others. Now it was too late—for Bixby! He had dug his own grave. Let him lie in it!

She was safe. Completely safe. Her heart skipped a beat. That scribbled message on the blue report! Almost instantly she smiled. No one had seen it but Ellen and herself. Ellen might not even have read it. If she had, that "p and m" could have meant nothing to her.

Better, of course, to recover the message from the pocket of the Peruvian doll and destroy it. If Mademoiselle saw it she would know what "p and m" meant. But if she made no effort to retrieve the note, even Mademoiselle would think nothing of it. Better to wait. If it came her way naturally, that was the time to act.

Dana rose and strolled across the picnic grounds to the gate, strolled down the path through the orchards. Occasionally she stopped to examine laden trees, to prune away a deformed apple here and there, straighten a prop supporting a branch.

She did not think consciously of Rick. She did not need to. Assured of her safety, she felt increasingly, too, his nearness to her, physically and emotionally.

When she came at last to the graveled drive she saw her husband waiting for her at the top of the terrace steps. He was smiling, amused. He must have been watching her attentions to the apple trees.

"Hi, farmer!" he greeted her. "I was about to call out the state police Dad's been telling me about. Have a good walk? You look tired."

She smiled up at him before mounting the steps. "And hot. And thirsty, too, I hope. What about you?"

"Dad and I have had quite a day. Exploring the fishing grounds. Tomorrow we begin a systematic campaign. Look here. I invited the whole family to dinner tonight for a distribution of the loot. That all right with you? I like them. I think they like me." His deep voice was warm with pleasure.

"For dinner, perfect. For the gifts—" She shook her head. "I've missed two Christmases with them, you know. I want to make it a real fiesta—tree and all. You don't mind?"

He chuckled, gave her arm an indulgent pat. "You infant! Not a bit. On the contrary. I've a number of Christmases to catch up on myself. When's the great event to be? How about next Saturday?"

"Whenever you like. You settle the date with the family while I shower." She stopped before a side entrance, waved a hand at Dock watching them from the east terrace. Shook her head when he made signs to her to hurry.

"Don't take too long," Coyne also advised as he opened the screen door for her, "We're about to have a visitor."

"A visitor! Who?"

"Someone named Carl Evoans. From the FBI. Federal Bureau of Investigation to you."

She turned, her foot on the step. "What makes him think he'll find investigation good here?"

Coyne chuckled. "I told him when he phoned he was an optimist. He's after that Bixby of yours. Seems that

Dock—others too—have reported the fellow for spreading subversive rumors. That's treason, or something, in time of war—"

At her startled expression he added, "Don't worry. By the time Dock and Dad get through telling this Evoans what they know about Bixby there won't be much left for you to say. You haven't had a chance to see the man yet, have you?"

Dana forced her voice to one more effort, but it was dry and cold. "Bixby? No, but I'd like to. I've been looking for him—"

Coyne smiled as he looked at her set face. "Dock said he'd hate to be in his shoes when you discovered what he'd done to your pools. Evidently you have."

He let the screen close after her. "Forget about Bixby. I'll handle him."

11

Monday Evening, July 28

The poker-faced young man whom Dock brought to the east terrace an hour later looked slightly abashed when he was introduced to Dana. His interview with Dad and Mother Madison had not prepared him for this fragile, exotic creature, smiling faintly from the depths of a padded chaise longue. The shining blond hair, usually swept back in sophisticated rolls from her face, now lay in soft curls, restrained by a bit of ribbon. Folds of a chiffon house gown in orchid shades emphasized the delicate lines of her body and her amethyst eyes.

He turned from her quickly to take with more assurance the hard but friendly hand Coyne extended. Then, glancing about in the momentary silence that followed, he spied a light chair.

"I'm sorry to break in on your evening like this, Mrs. Coyne," he apologized as he lifted it closer to her side. "But perhaps I won't have to take much of your time. You know why I'm here?"

"I told her," Coyne informed him.

"Your father and brother have already given me a good deal of information about this Bixby," the FBI agent went on without pausing. "I understand from them that during the first two years you employed him—that is, while you were living here yourself—he was perfectly satisfactory, both as a superintendent and as a man."

At her almost imperceptible nod he continued, "But during these past two years—in your absence—he has changed. Become arrogant, overbearing, inefficient—"

"My wife can't answer that question from any personal knowledge yet," Coyne interposed warningly. "She hasn't had time to see the fellow."

"But he was here this noon, wasn't he, Mrs. Coyne?"

"A maid—Ellen—saw him when he came," Dana corrected in her low, throaty voice. "I did not."

"That was when he sent you the message to meet him at 5 p.m. sure?"

"He what?" Coyne demanded.

"Sounds just like him," Dock commented.

"He did write something like that—across the bottom of a report he sent in to me by Ellen," Dana admitted.

"So Ellen says. You agreed to meet him?"

"Certainly not. I didn't answer him. I was busy with my children." Her pale face lighted and she turned to her husband. "Darling, you should have stayed to see them open the gifts we brought them. They were thrilled—"

With a small gesture of apology she turned back to Evoans. "I'm sorry. I think I was annoyed when I saw that note. But I didn't really read it. Just saw it. In my children's happiness—and my own to be with them again after two years—I really didn't think much about it."

Evoans nodded. "Sure. I can imagine. I've got youngsters of my own."

They smiled slowly at one another.

"When their Mademoiselle came to prepare them for their luncheon," Dana told him then, "I remembered that note. But the report was lost in the tissue paper and things. I called—that is, I had her—the governess—call Bixby. I was going to have her tell him I'd see him at my convenience—tomorrow. He wasn't home. His daughter said she didn't expect him to return until he'd seen me—at five."

Coyne moved irritably in his chair. Evoans nodded. "Yes, that's what she—Mary Bixby—told me."

"And that's about all I know," Dana concluded. "Except that after lunching with my mother I went for a walk around my grounds. Before I talked with Bixby I wanted to see how he'd carried out instructions I'd left with him."

She paused, her eyes darkening. "He hadn't done anything I wanted. Nothing. Worse than nothing."

"You didn't run into him anywhere?"

She shook her head.

Mr. Evoans cleared his throat. "Where were you this afternoon at five, Mrs. Coyne?"

Her eyes opened on his in helpless astonishment. Coyne chuckled. "Time and my wife are strangers, Mr. Evoans. If it's important for you to know we'll have to dig for the answer."

"I'd like to know, sir."

"*Paciencia,* then. Dock, will you call Mother Madison? Find out what time Dana left her. I'll check up here."

"Mademoiselle," Dana said suddenly. "She might know what time I left on my walk. I talked with her for a moment."

Mrs. Coyne, Mademoiselle said promptly when called, had left the house just after five. Her eyes met Dana's for an instant, the shadow of a smile in them.

"And the appointment was for five? Here," Evoans commented. "Then Bixby never appeared to keep it?"

No, Mademoiselle told him. She and the children had been on the lawns from four until almost six. If he had come they must have seen him.

"Thank you." Mr. Evoans closed the little book in which he had made some notes, snapped a rubber band about it, and rose.

"It looks to me," he announced crisply, "as if our bird had flown. That appointment business is an old gag. Impressed on everyone's mind that he was around somewhere, would be until after five. In the meantime, he skipped. By train from Hanotak to New York, probably."

"You think he had some warning you were coming?" Coyne asked.

"Looks like it, doesn't it?" Evoans nodded his head thoughtfully. "But we'll get him. His skipping out this way makes me think more than subversive rumors can be laid at his door."

For a moment he studied the house wall, then asked, "Your home has been closed for two years, Mrs. Coyne? Bixby had the keys, I suppose."

Dana nodded. "During the winters the house had to be heated—that is, kept to a temperature of sixty-five. Bixby took care of that."

Evoans' next question startled them with its remoteness from any thought in their minds. "How far's this place from the Sound?" He looked at Dock.

"Not quite twenty miles."

"See any signs—when you opened it just now—that someone might have occupied it for a time?"

Their blank looks answered him. Dock's changed to understanding. He pursed his lips in a soundless whistle.

"Well, I guess that's all. Until we find him." Evoans tucked his notebook away, picked up his hat. With brief farewells to Dana and Coyne he turned away. Dock went with him to his car.

Dana sank back in her chair, closed her eyes. Coyne pushed a bell beside the doors.

"Coming right up," he told her as he walked over to seat himself on the foot of her chair. "With that word 'subversive' hanging over us, I was afraid to offer the poor guy a drink."

She lifted her heavy lashes to smile at him. "What did those questions about the house mean?"

"Let's wait for Dock. He'll know." Coyne waved the question aside. "Now, I'm about to assume my role as heavy husband. From today on, you're to forget all about this place except to enjoy it. I'm taking over. I'll have those woods cleaned out, restore those pools—"

"No! No!" She sat up, then sank back. A long shudder ran over her. "I never want to see or hear of them again."

"Now, now, trifle," he cautioned indulgently. "You take things too hard. By spring you'll feel differently."

"Spring? Next spring?"

"Best time to clean out woods is in the winter," he began, then at the sound of voices rose with alacrity. "Here comes my nice new family. Hi, Dad!"

Mother Madison and Daphne followed slowly, Daphne lagging to wait for her husband, rounding the house from the drive.

"Whew!" Dock caught them up with an arm about each, swept them onto the terrace. "Gather round, everybody. I've been putting two and two together."

He waited until a maid, wheeling out a portable bar, had placed it before Coyne and departed.

"Evoans," he said then, "wasn't giving anything away. But he did ask that we keep our eyes and ears peeled for anything else on Bixby. It's my guess he thinks Bix may have been mixed up someway in the landing of those Nazi saboteurs on Long Island. Possibly that he sheltered one or more in this house for a time. The dumb cluck—Bixby, I mean—to disappear—"

"Why dumb?" asked his practical wife.

"Because now they'll hang everything on him. Though, personally, I think he talked too much for even Nazis to trust."

"Well, he's gone," Dad Madison said comfortably. "That solves our problem. The rest's up to this Evoans. Nice fellow. Smart, too." He stopped as Mademoiselle appeared round the house.

"Yes?" Dana asked when the governess approached her chair.

"I was looking for my stick, madame. I always walk after the children are in bed."

"Mademoiselle!" Dana was contrite. "I'm so sorry. I must have left it somewhere. Take one of mine if they're unpacked. I'll look for yours tomorrow."

"Thank you, madame." The governess's voice was courteous enough, but her glance and back as she turned away were stiff with displeasure.

12

Tuesday Morning, July 29

As the little Swiss bell on her sitting-room door tinkled Dana drew a mirror from beneath the piled-up pillows on her bed for a final survey of herself. Her hair falling in soft curls about her face, her cheeks and lips faintly pink, her short, straight nose faintly shining were satisfactory.

Except for the tightness about her eyes she looked, in fact, positively dewy. To soften their hard shine, she blinked her lashes rapidly while she fluffed the gay, filmy bed jacket about her shoulders.

When the bell tinkled again she thrust the mirror away, called, "Come in, darlings."

She heard her sitting-room door open, a blur of footsteps on the rugs there, but only Mademoiselle entered the bedroom. Behind her in the doorway, hand in hand, stood a sober Bunny and Whiffles.

"Come in, angels." Dana flung out her arms to them. "I can't wait for my good morning."

As they continued to stand motionless, regarding her with unblinking eyes, she turned questioningly to the governess.

"They are disappointed, madame, because you did not say good night to them last night." Dana thought she detected both pleasure and resentment in Mademoiselle's low tones.

"Oh, that wretched man!" she cried. "Bring Bunny in, Whiffles, and I'll explain. I couldn't come to you last night, darlings. A man came and stayed and stayed. When he went away at last, you were fast asleep."

"Who?" Whiffles demanded.

"Just a man—on business. Come in and forgive me, sweets."

Bunny, the Peruvian doll wife dangling by an arm from her free hand, broke from Whiffles to run in and climb up on the bed. Before snuggling, sniffing with pleasure, into the fragrant folds of the bed jacket, she took time to place the doll tenderly on a tiny lace pillow.

Whiffles followed slowly. At the bed he accepted his mother's kiss unresponsively, then stood back, his eyes still skeptical.

"What is it, precious?" Dana coaxed.

He hesitated, looked first at Mademoiselle. "Perhaps—you didn't mean what you said—about the case, either."

The mature and careful way he spoke testified to the length and frequency of his talks with Dad Madison.

"The case? Oh, for our collection? But of course I did."

Whiffles slid a small, triumphant smile at Mademoiselle, drew closer to lean against Dana's shoulder, his small nose crinkling, too, with pleasure.

"But he said, madame," Mademoiselle explained doubtfully, "he could choose the place to display the beetles. And he wants the case hung above the fireplace in the living room."

"What a marvelous idea! The perfect place, of course." Dana overrode the governess's misgivings with such warm approval that, all barriers removed, Whiffles' shining glance returned.

"Where is the case, then?" he wanted to know. "Can I get it now?"

"Of course. Take the children to the attic, Mademoiselle. You'll find the big chest there that belonged to Fretz Dreier. The cases should be in it or near it. Perhaps Bunny can find something she'd like too."

Whiffles was off like an arrow. Bunny, the doll forgotten, rolled off the bed with practiced accuracy to race after him. When Mademoiselle made no move to follow, Dana asked impatiently, "Yes? What is it?"

"Mr. Coyne, madame. He would like to see you before he goes."

"Tell him I'm awake now, please."

Mademoiselle turned away but paused in the sitting-room door to say, "It is not necessary that you search for my stick, madame. Mr. Coyne found it this morning."

Dana looked after her, irked again by the governess's voice and manner. When she heard the sitting-room door close she lay back thoughtfully on her pillows.

Rick hadn't taken the cane with him then! Had he dropped it in that little clearing, forgotten it, as she had, when he took her in his arms? She smiled but thrust the thought aside. She'd think of Rick when everyone was gone. Enough now to have that tingling assurance of his nearness underlying every moment.

Mademoiselle was the one to think about now. Had she only imagined some cool reserve, watchfulness, in the woman's manner? The governess had been displeased the night before because her cane had been mislaid. But that was a characteristic reaction of her meticulous soul.

She could not remember that Mademoiselle had ever looked directly at her when she spoke. Certainly her eyes had been averted just now when she mentioned the cane. But that might have been because her attention was on the children.

The tinkling bell interrupted her speculations. As her husband entered she noticed the doll, forgotten, on the pillow. She picked it up, but he gave her no chance to look at it.

"Morning, orchid," he greeted her, and his face was serious as he approached the bed. "Sure you feel up to this devoted-mother role? It goes over big, I know. But is it really necessary to dramatize every meeting with your young?"

Her eyes grew wishful as she looked up into his dark face. "I want them always to remember me as the loveliest thing in their lives."

"Remember? Aren't thinking of leaving us, are you?" His amused smile stopped midway. "Listen, Cinderella. We're home. Home to stay. And, God, is it good! I spent most of the night planning how to unload this and that onto others so I can handle things from here."

Seizing a low chair as he talked, he swung it round beside her. "We can do wonders with this place, trinket. It's got everything—location, woods, water. The soil's not much for farming, but for—"

At her astonishment he explained, "I was up with the sun. Before breakfast had tramped over the whole place. And by the way, I found that cane of Mademoiselle's. On a sort of path that runs from the picnic grounds to a nice little clearing."

"I came home that way," she said quickly.

"So I noticed." He cocked a surprised eyebrow at her. "You've got a touch of mountain goat in you no one would suspect. But that path—and the cane—are one of the reasons why I'm here. I'll ask Dad's man—Pete, isn't it?—to clean up those paths. But until further notice I want you to keep out of the woods."

Across her face that had grown still as he talked flicked one of the piquant glances that pleased him. "My heavy husband, I've roamed those woods since I was a child."

"But you're not a child now. These last seven or eight years have made you physically and mentally brittle. And that trip around South America, the life you led, our flight home—they were no rest cure, either. You took only a short walk yesterday—I could follow your trail by your heel marks. Yet you were white as a chased rabbit when you returned. I want to fish with a calm mind—not imagining you somewhere in the woods with a broken ankle."

She flicked another glance at him. "It's not broken ankles entirely, is it?"

"You mean snakes?" He shook his head. "No. I know those babies. They like sun—dry ground, rocks. They aren't in your north woods, though they may be in the high grass around that stagnant pond. I didn't see any. I saw deer tracks, though. Fox tracks too." His look implied more.

"Rabbits? There used to be pheasants."

"Well, two-legged foxes, if you must know. Looks as if some man's been making himself at home around that pond."

Dana sat up, biting back the name on her lips.

"Bixby?" he asked, misreading her thought. "No. I've got his heavy boot marks spotted. He's been there recently, but he's not the one I mean. This fellow's left tracks to the pond from the road and back again. He's as tall but lighter than Bixby. Takes a shorter stride. Wears sports shoes—rather an unusual kind."

Dana's small white teeth flashed as she laughed. "You'll tell me next the color of his eyes! What have I married? Tarzan?"

He laughed with her. "Don't know about his eyes. But I can tell you he's a blond. Almost as fair as you. You didn't catch sight of him yesterday, I suppose?" She shook her head.

"No? I didn't think you did. He was there after you left. His tracks cover yours everywhere. Almost as if—"

When her eyes fixed on him incredulously he added, "You've married a woodsman, my little rabbit. And he's telling you to keep out of the woods until they're safe for little rabbits. I met Mademoiselle on the path where I found the stick. She was searching for it too. She had only to look at it to understand why I told her to stay on the lawns near the house and keep the children there too."

He rose to replace the chair by the window. Dana released her breath carefully.

"I hate serials. Go on."

"Can't say much more—yet. This fellow may be some harmless hick from the neighborhood with a fancy for your woods and pond. Or he may be the village idiot. At any rate, he didn't like your having visited his favorite haunts—"

13

Tuesday Morning, July 29

Tumult in the corridor, then in the sitting room, interrupted him. Whiffles and Bunny tumbled through the doorway breathlessly, each crying, "Mine! Mine! Mummy, it's mine!"

"I foun' it," Bunny shrieked at sight of Dana.

"It's my father's!" Whiffles shouted her down.

Mademoiselle appeared behind them, carrying a unique golden box that seemed to be the issue. The children, Coyne, too, pressed round her as she took it to the bed, held it before Dana.

"Bunny found this in the chest inside another box; But, madame, you know what it is! It's much too valuable for a child to have."

Coyne leaned closer with sudden interest to inspect it. Straightening, he said, "Looks as if Mademoiselle is right, Jim."

"I don't want the old box," Whiffles told him. "Bunny can have it. But look! Show him, Mam'selle."

The governess had placed the box on the bed beside Dana. Instantly the late-morning sunshine made a brilliance of its heavily gilded baroque carving. As it stood on short, ornately carved and gilded legs, it appeared like a miniature chest itself, rounded in body and with a rounded, domelike top. Slipping a little catch at one side, Mademoiselle lifted the lid.

Contents of the box were then visible but still inaccessible because of a plate of glass that sealed the opening like an inner lid. Beneath the glass, fixed in place against what might have been white velvet but now appeared gray, were seven large, glittering beetles.

The hastiest glance proved them no ordinary species. Their life-size bodies were exquisitely worked from gold. Their heavy wings gleamed in different enamels, green, black, blue, inky purple. The eyes of each were jewels to match the wings in color.

Coyne was the first to note that though there were eight indentations there were only seven beetles. He was also the first to realize that Dana had not moved or spoken. She lay back on her pillows, her long lashes fluttering on pale cheeks.

"What is it?" he asked anxiously. "Mademoiselle, take the children—"

"No!" Dana opened her eyes, sat up, forcing her lips to smile. "I—I'd forgotten that box was in the house. It's very valuable. I meant to put it in a bank vault—thought I had—"

Her voice steadied, and her smile became more natural. "It belonged to Fretz—to Whiffles' father. The Dutch government, I think, presented it to him. There's an inscription inside the cover that tells. He—he found something here—invented some sort of powdered serum that they use in Ceylon or the East Indies somewhere for—I don't remember much about it—but it killed some pest there, I think."

Mademoiselle's head rose proudly. "The box was presented to Professor Dreier, Mr. Coyne, because he wouldn't take any money for what he did. As his special field of study was beetles, these jeweled replicas were made for him—"

"And they're mine, aren't they?" Whiffles interrupted, all impatience.

The governess shook her head, but Dana assured him quickly, "Yes. Yes, of course they're yours, darling."

"And I can take them out, can't I? I want them in the case we found up there. I want them to be with my—our—collection."

His greedy little hand reached for the box. Mademoiselle again moved to protest. Dana, a restraining hand on Whiffles, looked questioningly at her husband.

"He could do that, couldn't he? After all, the case can be locked. No one would expect to find anything so valuable in it."

Coyne looked up from his absorbed study of the jeweled insects. "It's your pidgin, my dear. Yours and Jim's. But those beetles are made of pure gold. Their eyes are small but perfect, emeralds, rubies, sapphires."

He smiled suddenly, placed a finger on a minute lock. "Guess this is all pretty academic anyway. Doesn't look as if it were meant to be opened."

Dana nodded reassurance at the crestfallen Whiffles. "There's a key, of course, precious, somewhere. I'll find it. In the meantime, you can have the box in your own room."

Bunny, listening silently, her small face growing stormier at each word, clutched at the box as Mademoiselle lifted it from the bed. "Mine!" she shrieked. "Mine! I foun' it."

In a rage she snatched the Peruvian doll from Dana's lap, hurled it to the floor. Howling like a small fury, she began to jump up and down on it.

Hurriedly Mademoiselle placed the box in Whiffles' arms, lifted Bunny, and bore her, sobbing and kicking, from the room. Whiffles followed close behind, nursing his treasure but shouting promises of other possessions of his Bunny could have instead. Coyne rescued the doll.

Dana made no protest at their going. Her eyes were focused on her husband, turning the doll in his hands, testing its movable legs and arms.

A thread of delft blue against the black wool skirt attracted his attention. Smiling, he drew it from the tiny pocket. “Look at this!” he exclaimed, holding it out on his palm.

She lowered her eyes slowly. On his hand lay a blue handkerchief, no larger than a postage stamp.

Her veiled glance grew suddenly bright, then intent, as she leaned forward and picked it up. It was made of silk, its edges fringed.

14

Tuesday Afternoon, July 29

For some time after everyone had gone Dana could not think of Rick. The governess again held her attention. Obviously Mademoiselle had seen that crumpled bit of blue paper in the Peruvian doll's pocket, understood the message. More: she must have taken it and, to pacify Bunny's possessiveness, made a blue handkerchief of silk to replace it.

It was possible that Bunny, carrying the doll about, had lost the scrap of paper, demanded another—of blue. But if so, how could Mademoiselle have known to select a shade that matched so closely?

Irritably Dana fussed with the question, finding no answer that satisfied her. Finding no answer, either, to justify the nervous alarm she was feeling.

At last she thrust thought of the handkerchief from her mind, lay back, her eyes fixed unseeingly on the ceiling. Little by little her tension left her. She lay relaxed among the pillows, a luxurious smile tilting her lips. Only a few more hours and she would be with Rick!

Memory of her husband's warning to stay out of the woods brought her upright. Carter Coyne's keen eyes more than his words convinced her that she could not meet Rick in the clearing. Filled with sudden energy, she jumped up to bathe and dress.

On light feet she left her rooms, sped down the long corridor to the living room. As she went she became conscious of the stillness of the house.

"Where are the children?" she asked Ellen, arranging flowers in the living room.

"Mademoiselle has taken them for luncheon and the afternoon with Dr. Madison's boys, Mrs. Coyne. I believe she said it was a custom for them to spend Tuesday together."

Dana's irritation at not being informed fled. "Splendid," she said. "I'll have my luncheon on the terrace at one or so. Tell Sardaki, will you? And ask Bowen to have the car here for me at three. Tell him I'll drive myself."

She stopped, half smiling at the unconcealed admiration in the maid's eyes.

The girl flushed a little. "Excuse me, madame. I—I was just thinking you look sort of lit up—like a bride. So pretty, I mean."

Dana laughed, a note of excitement in her pleasure. "Thank you, Ellen. It's because I'm home again, perhaps."

She turned casually toward the stairway. "You've reminded me I'm the mother of two children. And should do something about it. While I have a moment I'll look at their floor."

As casually she mounted the stairs, but in the children's suite above, the doors to the corridor closed, her nonchalance vanished. Swiftly but thoroughly she searched their rooms and baths, seizing on anything that showed a glint of delft blue.

Nothing. Nothing in either bedroom that resembled a bit of blue paper bearing a scribbled line in pencil. Nothing in the huge sunlit playroom among the neat racks of toys. Nothing used as a bookmark in the books on shelves and tables. Nothing on the play porch outside, either.

For a time she stood at the broad railing there, looking out across the grounds to the woods that concealed the old Hedley farmyard. What must it be like now with Rick in charge? And what had brought Rick back to farm the old place? She smiled to herself. He wouldn't need to farm—any longer. He wouldn't need to look so fine-drawn, so disciplined, any longer.

She tore her eyes from the view and her thoughts from Rick to study her own grounds with delight. All this was hers—the lawns with their maples, hickory, fir, and spruce, their gardens and flowered walks, this house, the orchards, the woods.

Her eyes rested covetously first on Dock's green-shingled home, then on her father's. She'd like to own them, too, but Daphne was capable of forcing Dock to move. If he went Dad and Mother Madison might go with them.

No, better to leave the arrangement as it was. Build the life she wanted with the support of a solid family front. She wouldn't change a shingle or a blade of grass. The place had a settled, established look now, with the trees and shrubbery grown. Even she, vivid as were her memories of the rambling farmhouse and yard that once stood here, could hardly realize how different it had all appeared once.

As Carter had said, they could do wonders with the place. She smiled again. He had meant with the farms. The farms meant nothing to her except as possessions. Carter was going to do much more, though neither he nor she had realized it—in Bogota. She had counted then on his money, his name. Not until they reached New York had she learned how many people he knew, what people he knew.

Her gaze lifted again to travel far beyond the Hedley woods to see with her mind's eye the tall towers of Amery Chimneys on the other side of the valley. A slow, triumphant little smile lighted her face.

It vanished as a young girl in shorts ran out of the white cottage just inside the main gates. Mary Bixby! She'd forgotten about the child. She must do something about her soon.

She was turning away when she caught sight of Mademoiselle hurrying out of Dock's gates and across the lawns to meet Mary. Curious, she moved back to the rail, stood watching.

Before the two met Mary was already gesturing excitedly, angrily. Mademoiselle hastened her steps. She put her arms around the girl, bent her head, obviously trying to calm and reassure her. Then slowly the two started back toward the superintendent's cottage.

With sudden resolution Dana turned to the playroom doors, then hurried on to the governess's own room. For a moment she stood in its doorway, her eyes fixed in disapproval on the austerity and order there. Though comfortably, even luxuriously, furnished, it gave no sign that anyone occupied it. Except for the cane lying across the foot of the bed, not a personal thing was visible.

Dana's eyes widened as she moved closer to look at the stick. The ram's horn was not polished now. It was dull and curiously scratched and battered. As she recalled Rick's use of it, her brows wrinkled in perplexity. Nothing she could remember explained the punishment it had clearly suffered. But this, then, explained in part Mademoiselle's coolness, her husband's warning.

Uneasily she straightened, looked about the room, with quick decision began to search it. Only a minute or two were necessary for the room itself. Not even a personal letter marred the order of the desk. Nowhere there or in the bath was there anything blue. Mademoiselle, she remembered, never wore bright colors any more. Blacks, grays, dull greens.

Opening the door of the deep clothes closet, she saw her memory confirmed in the line of dresses and coats suspended precisely on hangers. Nothing in any pocket. Nothing on the shoe shelf below, the hat shelf above.

She pulled forward a small chest and after a momentary hesitation opened it. The contents brought spots of unaccustomed color to her face. In shining white boxes, carefully wrapped, lay bibs, dresses, baby shoes, toys of Bunny and Whiffles. In albums, photographs, snapshots of the children, singly and together—book after book. Beneath them, in more shining boxes, gifts the children had given their governess. Cards, printed sketchily in crayon by Whiffles, lay inside each one.

As she opened one she caught her breath. Blue showed beneath the white tissue paper, and the card bearing Bunny's wriggles and conception of the greatest amount of anything in the world—"I love you 2½."

Her breath caught again as she turned back the tissue paper. Beneath it lay a delft-blue scarf. Staring back at her like an empty eye was a neat square hole, no larger than a postage stamp!

With cool fingers she replaced the tissue, closed the box, and returned it to the chest and the chest to its place. She did not need to look farther for the bit of blue paper. Mademoiselle had it. Mademoiselle considered it so valuable that to secure it she had sacrificed a scarf given her by Bunny!

But why? To what possible use could the woman intend to put it? She must have had it yesterday afternoon, yet she had said nothing to correct Evoans' impression that the appointment was for 5 p.m. at the house.

Thoughtfully Dana closed the room door, descended the stairs, ate her luncheon. But two hours later, when she slipped under the wheel of the closed car Bowen brought round for her, she was smiling.

"Remember, Mrs. Coyne, about the gas rationing," the chauffeur warned. "Three gallons a week—and this is

Tuesday. Though Bixby, I hear, has a storage tank almost full—"

She turned to look at the bronzed young man standing beside the opened door. "What about Bixby?"

"He had an X card. He got it because he did all the buying, he said, for these three places, used gas in the tractor and mowers." Bowen's ears clearly had not been idle since his arrival Sunday night. "If he's gone, Mr. Coyne probably can get his card."

As Dana nodded, started to put the car in gear, he added hurriedly, "You will stop to see Mary Bixby, perhaps?"

With an effort she sat back, controlling her impatience. "I hadn't intended to—today. Why?"

His honest brown eyes showed embarrassment. "I saw her last night, Mrs. Coyne. She's very worried there, alone. And she can't believe her father's run away. He took nothing with him, she says, not even money. And he was wearing his ordinary work clothes."

Dana was tapping the wheel lightly, thinking. "What's Mary like, Bowen? I've not seen her for two years, you know."

"She's not much more than a kid yet. Just seventeen. But she's a very sensible girl, Mrs. Coyne. Not hysterical like many would be. I never saw her father, but I don't think she's had a very happy life keeping house for him."

At Dana's smile he stopped, his ears reddening.

"Thank you, Bowen. You've given me an idea. Suppose you have another talk with her this afternoon—unofficially, of course. Find out what she'd like to do—if her father doesn't return. About relatives, if any, and so on. I ought to have some plan in mind before I talk with her. Tomorrow sometime—if she can come over."

She sped away from his appreciative eyes. In Hanotak half an hour later she bought armfuls of gay wrapping papers, bolts of ribbon, and made a telephone call. Then, slowly, savoring expectancy, she started back on the road she had come.

More than halfway home it curved to run between ranks of closely planted firs. Shortly a little-used side road, lined on either side with natural woods, joined it. She turned the heavy car into it, proceeded carefully over its narrow course until two stone pillars of a gateway loomed ahead.

With only a glance for the tall, fair man standing inside, she swung the car round and in. Another moment and he was beside her, opening the door as she stopped.

She dropped her hands from the wheel, turned as he slipped into the seat beside her. His arms went round her, tightened, as she lifted her face to his.

15

Tuesday Afternoon, July 29

It was Dana who released herself. Pushing him gently back, she studied his fine head, the sensitive features disciplined now, sophisticated.

"Tell me about this new Rick," she urged. "You're really different, aren't you? And I can't stay long."

His slow nod halted midway as her last words penetrated. "You can't stay? You are staying! Never to go again."

"You were the one who went away. I've never really gone, Rick. I'll never leave you, really."

He stopped her with a gesture. His voice with its faint foreign inflection spoke with slow bitterness. "Those are lip words, my Dana. You know why I went away. So that I could come back to you with something to—"

He stopped himself there, began again. "We are children no longer. Let us pretend no longer. I have been alone nine years. In nine years I have known all the ways there are to be alone. Now I come back. I have waited for you to come back too."

She turned from him to look out through the quivering green, uneasiness clouding her eyes, gripping her.

"Rick, please. Talk to me. About you. You never wrote. No one ever spoke of you again. When I heard your violin Sunday night I—I wouldn't let myself believe it might be yours." Her tone lightened. "How well you play now."

"So they say." His amused glance for her became amazement. Far back in his somber gray eyes a sparkle glinted.

"About me there is nothing," he told her solemnly. "I go to Europe. To Norway, first. I play my violin. I play and play—for nine years. Then comes the war. Of what use is a fiddler in a war? They say to me, 'You are American. Go home.' Voila! Here I am. Still playing my fiddle."

He tossed the years aside with a light swing of his lean, delicately formed hands. "But you, my Dana—oh, much has happened to you! You have not been alone."

"Too much has happened. Yet nothing, really, Rick. And I have been alone—always. As if—as if everything happened to upper layers of me while I—your Dana—waited underneath."

"We will forget the Dana of the upper layers. And talk about my Dana. About my Dana and me." He took her hand, turned back a slender finger. "Begin. One—"

"But you must know," she protested. "Everyone knows—"

"I know only from evidence visible to my own eyes that you have been married twice. Before I come back to this old farm I have this and that done. I add a swimming pool—just a simple one, of course—and to it, like bees to a flower, came the children from across the road. Then I come. I find them there. Dock's two boys. That is very well. Then came a little boy. His eyes are blue as wild asters, but like yours too. And a small girl with stormy ways—like yours. One says, 'I am Whiffles Dreier.' The other, 'Me Bunny Amery.'"

He brushed his free hand across his eyes before he turned, unsmiling, to look at her. "And I—I say, 'Your mother is Dana Madison, no?' Dock's twins say yes, I am right. Thunder and lightning strike me. I say to them, 'Go home! All of you. Never dare to come here again.' I frighten them very much because I am so frightened myself.

"Dock and Dad are very angry, of course, but I think they understand too. Never again do the children cross the road, come to the pool. No one crosses the road. I permit no one to enter my grounds. I talk with no one but my fiddle. My servants I bring from Norway. They are old and trustworthy. If they know anyone here they do not tell me. So—"

Dana remained silent, eyes averted. Obliquely Hedrick watched her as her tension relaxed and her slender lips quivered.

"Tell me, my Dana," he said gently then. "And tell me in your own voice, so clear and sweet. For others that acquired throb. For me, no."

"I was trying to find it—remember it," she confessed. "Oh, Rick, you're right! With each other we must be real. We can't pretend any more. But I can't find the real Dana. I've hidden her, protected her for so long, I can't reach her now. I'm not sure what the truth is. I'm lost, Rick! I can't find myself."

"God!" He took her in his arms again, rocking her gently. "Can't you forget that stupid hurt, my Dana? It's gone, years ago. Forgotten by all but you. Look at it. Laugh at it—"

"No, no," she protested. "It's not that, Rick. I haven't forgotten it. How could I? All my life since has been based on that Thanksgiving Eve. But it doesn't matter any more. I'm free of it." She sat up. Smiled at him meaningfully. "One day soon you'll see."

Rick shook his head. "To be exact, my Dana, your life, as you call it, began just forty-nine days before that Thanksgiving Eve. Surely you haven't forgotten the October day when Blake Amery, III, in his shiny red car, found us on our back road. Found you, rather. And came every day to carry you farther and farther away from the small world of Dock and Daphne and me—"

"No, I hadn't forgotten." Dana's voice was not throaty now. "I'll never forget, I hope. But it was Senator Amery—that night—who really changed my world or my way of looking at it. Whenever I've hesitated, been afraid to attempt something during these past years, I've only had to think of him standing there—like Zeus in a fury—warning my father to keep me away from his son."

She turned to caress him with her eyes, place her hand on his. "And to remember you—so shy and naive—shouting at him that I had no intention to marry his precious Blake—that I was going to marry you!"

"My one heroic moment—and you shattered it by flinging open the door and telling Zeus to go," Rick said dryly.

"And he went. That's what I mean. He had no right to come uninvited into our home, talk to my father like that. Yet he did. And—at least for a time—he got what he wanted. I hated and feared him that night—I still do. He's a ruthless, implacable old man. But I admired him too. And I decided then if that was the way to get what one wanted I'd be that way too. And I was. And I have—"

"At least for a time?" he qualified. "And assuming you knew what you wanted."

"For always," she declared. "You'll see. And I knew what I wanted. Blake had shown me that. It's the one thing I forgive him. Not money so much as the things money can do. Not a name cobwebby with traditions, but a name that means something *now.*"

"I see," he said gravely. He was silent, visualizing again that moment after the Senator had gone, when Dana, still enraged, hurled his violin into the fire, then herself into his arms. For an instant the sparkle shone again in his eyes.

"And this Fretz—Fretz Dreier," he asked carefully, following his thought, "was neither a poor farmer nor a poor fiddler? He had a name that means something now and—"

"We're simplifying too much, leaving too much unsaid. But it doesn't matter, does it? We've all the rest of our lives to talk. It took me months to make over the Dana of nine years ago into the Dana Dad sent to Cornell. Fretz was there—an exchange professor. I didn't think he was rich. I just knew he was someone pretty special. So—"

The corner of his lips quirked as he listened to her level, matter-of-fact voice, clear and cool, if not sweet. "The upper-layers Dana," he thought, "is talking now." In spite of his assurances to the contrary, his eyes fixed keenly on her.

"He was richer than I thought. When he died money came to me from Holland. I rebuilt Dad's and Dock's—all our houses—and with the rest went to New York. Blake Amery was there."

At some change in Rick she went on quickly, "I didn't love Fretz, but I was good to him. And I didn't hate Blake—at first. I didn't think about him, really. I think I thought more about his father, how he'd looked at us that night, what he'd said. I—I just wanted their money—to make them pay—"

She waited futilely. "That sounds cold, unfeeling, ruthless, doesn't it? Perhaps I was all three. But something snapped like a lock inside me that Thanksgiving Eve, Rick. As if the real me—and my love for you—were sealed over—locked away—safe from ever being hurt again. All that has happened since has happened to the upper-layers Dana—"

"Who interests me not at all." Rick waved away all she would say. "Now we begin—where we left off so many years ago. *Voila!* It is a summer afternoon, not a chilly winter night. About us are only quiet trees instead of a shouting Senator and a white-faced Dad. Otherwise—"

His light tone changed, deepened. "Now when I offer you myself and my fiddle—"

"No! No!" She drew away from him. "Rick, don't spoil everything now!"

"Spoil?"

"Understand me, Rick—you must. You always have. Isn't it enough that I love you—have always loved you—that we are together?"

His gaze searched her face, grew still. "No, it is not enough. Oh, I understand you, my Dana. We've both come a long way, grown very wise, haven't we, you and I? But I think you have not told me all the truth. We must begin again. Or, rather, you must tell me in simple words what lies between us now."

They sat motionless, almost expressionless, only their lips mobile. Hers moved, but no sound came from them.

He spoke for her. "It is not money still? Or my fiddle?"

"No. No, no."

"Nor—that I went away?"

She shook her head.

"Look at me, Dana." Anger rang in his voice. "It is not that you think of still a third—step?"

Her hands moved up, closed tightly about the wheel to quiet her inward shaking. "I—I have taken it," she murmured, almost inaudibly.

His stillness deepened. "So?" he said softly. "And your name now?"

"Mrs. Carter Coyne," she told him numbly, then spun around to face him. "But, Rick, you must understand. Listen—"

In one movement he was out of the car, standing with formal courtesy at the open door. "Understand, my Dana? But of course. It is not difficult at all. You are Mrs. Carter Coyne. You go now, Mrs. Coyne? The gate is open—like the door—nine years ago."

16

Tuesday Afternoon, July 29

Her hand firm on the wheel, Dana swung her car through the wide entrance to Madison Farms. But her eyes looked with wonder over the lawns where shadows of trees and shrubbery lengthened in the thinning afternoon sunlight.

How had she come here? From the moment Rick had turned his back, walked away, she had no memory of time or motion or changing scene. She only knew that her love for him, dammed back for so many years, was freed now. Free and pouring through her in a mighty flood, while at the thought of losing him she shook with cold. A horrible cold, heavy as a weight with cruelly jagged edges sinking slowly within her. She could have screamed with the sheer physical agony of its creeping progress.

Yet mentally she was oblivious to it. She would not lose him; she knew how to get him back; she would get him back. But "Wait, wait, wait," her lips were counseling the reckless urge of her mind.

As she rounded the last curve of the drive she saw Bowen running up from the garage to meet her. Automatically she switched on the glazed enamel facade she had learned would protect her from outside penetration of her mind and emotions.

Automatically she glanced in the mirror above her head. A smooth, pale face looked back at her, the same face she had seen when she left Bowen on the steps a few hours before. Reassured, she brought the car to a smart stop at the house door, left the engine running. With a smile Bowen opened the door, leaned in, and shut it off.

"I talked to Mary Bixby," he informed her immediately. "She has an aunt in California. But she doesn't want to leave here. Leave Hanotak, I mean. She wants to take a business course while—"

"While?" Dana heard herself repeat in a cool, clear voice.

"While she waits for her father to return. She still doesn't believe he's run away. And she seems more angry than alarmed—because of all the talk about him. She says—" Bowen hesitated. "She says someone must have sent him away. Since last Saturday, she told me, he's talked about money—a lot of money he expected to have soon."

Again Bowen paused. When Dana did not speak he added, "She's so stirred up now it's hard to reason with her. But it looks to me as if that FBI fellow may really have something on her father and she's just beginning to realize what it is. Anyway, she knows more than she'll say and she's frightened."

Dana registered each word he said but had no sense of hearing them. Something in her manner stopped the young man's eager flow. He drew back apologetically. "If it's convenient, Mrs. Coyne, Mary will come to see you tomorrow—about noon."

"Thank you." As Mademoiselle opened the house door Dana stepped from the car. Stepped carefully because of that dragging weight. While Bowen entered the car to collect her packages for the governess she slipped into the house and turned with relief down the corridor to her own door.

Inside, she leaned against it, waiting for that physical agony to lessen. Almost immediately, however, Mademoiselle was there. Dana watched her place the packages on a table, then moved toward her bedroom.

"Madame!"

The urgency packed into that one word swung her round. A glance at the governess's emotional stress alarmed her.

"What is it? Whiffles? Bunny?"

"No, no. I've just brought them home. Whiffles seems to have caught a light cold. They're in bed."

"Good. You startled me. Tell them I'm tired, too, going to bed. I'll see them in the morning. That's all, thank you, Mademoiselle."

"Madame!" the governess repeated in that same explosively repressed tone. "You were in my room before you left. Looking for something. Your perfume—"

With an effort Dana recalled her visit to the children's floor. But she had no will or strength to discuss it now. "Yes—just to see if everything was—all right."

"You found nothing—out of order." The words formed a statement rather than a question.

Dana's own tension found release in irritation. "On the contrary. Too orderly, Mademoiselle. It isn't necessary for the children—you, either—to be so neat. This isn't an institution, you know."

Anger flashed in the dark eyes, vanished. Mademoiselle said smoothly, "I find it best—with the children running in and out—not to leave personal things around."

Dana pulled off her hat, tossed it aside. While her drugged mind tried to understand the implication in Mademoiselle's words she massaged her forehead, thrusting back the damp curls. Her fingers suddenly pressed tight against her temples. That blue message! Was the tiresome woman trying to tell her further search was useless? Well, let her save her breath. She, Dana, knew it.

"You are ill, madame? You look very white. Let me get—"

"A slight headache, that's all. I should have worn sunglasses."

"I'm sorry. I—I had hoped we might talk a little, Mrs. Coyne. It is necessary, important, that we should. I am older than you, madame, have had more experience. I beg of you, let me advise—"

Dana bit back the mocking words that rushed to her lips. "Thank you. Not now, Mademoiselle."

As she turned to enter her bedroom she caught again that curious urgency in the governess's gaze. But her mind refused to consider Mademoiselle further. What did she, anyone, anything matter until Rick had been regained? Rick who had turned his back on her, walked away.

She walked heavily to her dressing table, sank down before it. After a moment she heard her sitting-room door close softly. She moved to rise, remembering that urgency, sank back. "Later. I'll talk with her later," she promised herself. "Now I must think about Rick. Rick comes first."

But her mind was a bleak, frozen blank. And the eyes looking back at her from the mirror were tight and bleak in an aching head.

The tinkle of her Swiss bell recalled her. Swiftly she seized a brush, was stroking it through her unbound hair when, after a pause, her husband entered.

"Just met Mademoiselle," he began anxiously. "She said you were ill." Coyne smiled, his eyes on her shining hair. "When you look like that I'm no judge."

"Only a headache, darling. If you don't mind having dinner alone, I'll try to sleep it off."

"Smart girl. About time you decided to take some rest. I'll just tuck the offspring in and amble over to Dad's. Perhaps I can wangle dinner from Mother Madison. And Dad and I might get some of our ideas about this place down on paper afterward."

"No!" Dana cried. "No!" At his surprise she shook her head wearily. "Dad's always had ideas about this place. Nothing ever came of them."

"Because he never had the means to carry them out. Nothing the matter with his ideas."

Coyne gave her one of his curiously shy, almost boyish grins. "I'm good medicine for your father, trinket. Haven't you noticed how he's bucked up? Voice stronger. More vitality. Maybe if I show him how to make his ideas click he'll snap out of it. Plus good medical attention, of course."

He tilted up her face with a finger. "What have you been up to, trifle? It isn't like you to be upset like this. No, don't answer. Hop into bed and I'll send you something to make you sleep."

Before his steady, penetrating gaze could pierce too deeply Dana turned away. But when Coyne did, too, an overwhelming impulse brought her to her feet. To tell him about Rick. To ask him to release her. He had said he would. She knew he would.

"Carter!"

But when he swung round, the discipline of years would not allow the words to cross her lips. She had worked so hard, endured so much. Now she had safety, security, the place in the sun she had dreamed of. She could not sacrifice it. There must be some other way.

"Yes?" Coyne prompted. "What is it, my dear?"

She shook her head. "Nothing. Unless—you'd like to know you're good medicine for me too, Carter."

He took a step toward her, his eyes warm with pleasure. "That's a leading remark, Dana. Want to tell me why?"

As her face veiled again he looked thoughtfully at her. "Look here. Has that governess—" Abruptly he stopped. "We'll talk tomorrow. Unless you'd like me to toss her out tonight."

"Mademoiselle?" Dana repeated stupidly. Her head was whirling now, her heart racing. She felt as if she had narrowly escaped stepping off a precipice. Lest her knees betray her, she sank down again on the seat of her dressing table.

"Oh, I know she's the sum of all the virtues," Coyne said, "but she's too emotional to have complete charge of children. In a place like this, at least, where she has no chance to release whatever's on her mind. I certainly didn't like the look on her face just now."

At the door he turned to say, "And this wasn't the first time today I've seen her leave these rooms looking like a cat that had trapped a mouse."

17

Tuesday Evening, July 29

When she was sure Coyne had gone Dana pushed herself to her feet, prepared hurriedly for bed. Thoughts of Mademoiselle's two visits to her rooms, of her husband, of the impulse to ask for her release, she held at bay. Time enough—time enough—to think of them.

Not until she lay shivering between the cool sheets did she release the brake she had placed on her thoughts and emotions. "Now I can think about Rick."

But Ellen entered then, a stiff, hot drink on her tray. While Dana drank it the maid moved about, putting things away, drawing curtains.

"Just let yourself go, madame," she advised as she took the glass and turned to leave. "You don't know it, but you're all tired out. Mr. Coyne's given orders no one is to disturb you." Quietly she closed the door behind her.

"Now," Dana murmured again. But now the hot drink or something her husband had placed in it swept her away into deep, drugged sleep.

Hours later, when she roused, the room was completely dark, the house silent. Yet some sound—some important sound—had called her back from sleep, was still ringing in her ears. She sat up, struggling to find and identify it.

Suddenly she was alert, out of bed, standing taut in the darkness, facing her open French doors. Clear and strong through the warm, quiet night came the resonant notes of a violin. Rick's violin! Rick playing as she had never heard him play before. Playing to her, for her! For a long moment she stood listening, responding.

Then feverishly she was dressing in dark slacks, shirt, and flat-soled Peruvian sandals. That dead, tearing weight was gone. She did not have to face the thought she had lost Rick! Did not have to face the nightmare of winning him back—by losing Carter and all Carter stood for.

Rick had forgiven her, understood her again, as he had so many times. This was his way of telling her. His way of coming to her, calling her to him!

She slipped out of the French doors and sped—a dark shadow—across the lawns toward Dock's house and the little gate there that opened onto the road. Like a shadow she sped past his lighted windows and out into the warm darkness.

A few rods above the gate an old side road opened on the left to the Hedley farm. In her heedless haste she had followed it some distance before she realized she had no need for the flat-soled sandals.

This was not the narrow, rutted road of the old days. Broad and smooth, palely white with sand, it wound through trees on either side that no longer formed a tangle of brush and woods.

As she hurried on she could see in some light radiating from the house ahead that she was moving through a carefully groomed park. From shrubs and bushes, faintly starred with flowers, drifted a strange, illusive fragrance.

She noted but took no time for thought. The violin and the hand that played it drew her like a magnet. She moved lightly, rhythmically, buoyed with delight and expectancy. Rick! Soon she would see him—perhaps could watch him a moment without his knowing—as he played for her!

The road swung sharply left. She stopped, bewildered, startled. High gates sealed it there, and a fence disappeared on either hand among the trees and darkness. Rick had prepared her for changes in the familiar farmyard between the rambling old house and the barns and sheds. But he had not prepared her for what her eyes now told her lay beyond the gates.

Lawns rolled away from the inner curve of the road to a low terrace that rose to another lawn. In its center an oval pool shimmered beneath soft lights concealed in trees. Dimly she was aware of a gray stone house farther to the left, guarded by more trees.

But her entire attention focused on the tall, lean figure, all in white, standing at one end of the pool. Cheek to violin, Rick stood there, one arm inscribing patterns on the air with the creamy pencil of his bow.

Rick, yet not the old shy Rick, the fiddler. He was lost in his music as always, but differently, completely differently. She knew little of music. Fretz had loved it, she remembered irrelevantly then, must have known deeply the feeling that gripped her now. She could not stir or take her eyes from that absorbed, swaying figure. Unaccountably it was she who felt shy.

Sound or movement near by startled her to turn. An old man, or oldish, at least, was stepping out of the deep shadow of trees inside the gates.

"Madame, I am sorry. It is forbidden for strangers to come here. Beside the road, yes. I permit the young people to enter. They love the music too. Not here."

His low, bass voice, touched with an accent similar to Rick's, broke the spell. "Nonsense," she said curtly. "I'm an old friend of Mr. Hedley's. He expects me. Open the gate."

"Mr. Hedley? But this is the home of Hedrick, madame. As you can see—and hear." Pride rang in his slow words as he gestured toward the pool.

"Hedrick?"

As clearly as if written in words on the darkness, she could read the amazement, even anger, in the sunken eyes regarding her. "Madame does not know of Hedrick? The great violinist of Norway, Europe, all the world?"

"Of course I know that Hedrick—"

She stopped, startled again. Frightened at the thought flashing through her mind.

"This is the home of Hedrick. He stands there—playing now. He prepares for his tour of the United States this winter and for the concerts he is to give soon in the Army camps." The deep voice grew stern. "Madame must go back."

The admonition was as unnecessary as the gate. Dana's stillness was so complete, her whole being so rocked at the discovery that Rick—her Rick—was Hedrick, she appeared rooted to the spot.

She could not doubt the old man's words. Rick Hedley. Hedrick. Of course. Why had she not guessed years ago when first she heard of the young genius of the violin discovered in Norway? Rick had gone to Norway.

As she gazed at Hedrick her wonder was still daunted. This disciplined man playing with such authority, Rick! The Rick she had not married, knowing he could never do anything but play a fiddle! Knowing it as late as this afternoon!

Her face burned as if stung, but her clenched hands were damp and cold. She forced herself to remain erect, composed, until she could speak and walk steadily.

"You are right," she said then. "This is not the home of Mr. Hedley. Good night."

"Good night, madame."

Slowly at first, then swiftly, she retraced her steps, closing her ears to the call of the violin. As she approached the outside road she was vaguely conscious of dim figures moving among the trees, of a young man and girl stepping aside to permit her to pass.

On the dark road once more, she stumbled forward, slow, dry sobs racking her. Terrifying her. But she went on, intent once more on reaching seclusion before she acknowledged the truth she would not face that afternoon. Now, indeed, she had truly lost Rick!

Mother Madison and Daphne, knitting on the lighted screen porch, heard those racking sobs before Dock, absorbed in a newspaper near them, looked up. They turned toward the road, rose.

"It's Dana!" Daphne exclaimed, peering out. "Dock, it's Dana."

In one stride Dock reached the light switch, plunged the porch in darkness. "Stay here, Mother. You too, Daph. Don't let her see us see her."

"But something's wrong." On her way to the door Mother Madison paused reluctantly. "Dana never cries. She can't cry."

Daphne moved quickly to the older woman's side. Silently they watched the slender dark figure pass through the gate, continue blindly round the walk and out of sight. After a moment Dock switched on the lights, flung himself into a chair.

"God help us all," he said fervently. "I never thought I'd see the day when I could pity Dana. But I'd give my right arm to help her now. She came from Rick's. She knows—"

"—he's Hedrick," Daphne finished for him. "Well, she had it coming," she mused practically. "I'm glad it's over. And she's survived worse things. She'll get over this."

Dock gave her a long, odd glance, then looked at his mother.

She nodded uneasily. "I was thinking of Carter too," she said.

18

Wednesday Morning, July 30

But when Mother Madison and Daphne hurried over the next morning they found a gay and carefree Dana sitting on the floor of the living room, deep in excitement and chaos. Before her the gilded baroque box containing the seven gold beetles gleamed in the sunshine. Like a Mexican jumping bean, Whiffles pendulated between her and Mademoiselle, also on the floor near by.

Before the governess lay a large opened specimen case, with beetles from Whiffles' own collection already ranged in neat rows about an empty oval in the center. On a sea of newspapers spread round her were others, each neatly impaled on its pin.

Her skilled fingers moved among them, selecting the best specimens to complete the background. The golden seven, as Whiffles proclaimed over and over, were to stand together in the oval in a single blaze of glory.

Dock's nine-year-old twins, Mark and Matt, clad in overalls, their reddish hair tousled, their brown feet bare, for once were motionless and wordless. Their mother had warned them that their usual garb would not do in their aunt Dana's house; now they knew it. But hardily they slouched together in a window, exchanging loud glances and subdued but succinct comments on the hullabaloo going on over a lot of dead beetles.

The only quiet spot in the room was Bunny. Pressed tight to Mademoiselle's side, she watched proceedings with stony eyes.

As her mother and sister-in-law entered, stood looking about in bewildered surprise, Dana waved a tiny gold key in greeting. "You're just in time for the grand opening," she cried. She rose to her knees to receive her mother's kiss, Daphne's sly pinch on her ear, then dropped back.

"Herewith I present you with the key, Whiffles darling. Now, open your box."

The boy's small fingers closed round the key, but he made no effort to place it in the lock. Stooping, he picked up the box, carried it to Mademoiselle.

"You open it, Mam'selle, please," he invited shyly. "Take the first look."

Color warmed the governess's face as she inserted and turned the key, lifted the glass top, and bent her head to look. "They're beautiful, Whiffles." Lifting the box, she placed it in his arms. "Don't you want to show them to everyone?"

Proudly he carried his treasure to Mother Madison. Her smile vanished as she looked. "Whiffles," she exclaimed in concern, "the black beetle has lost his little wife! Dana, how can that be? They were all there when I packed Fretz's things away."

"You're incorrigible, Mother." Daphne laughed as she placed an affectionate arm about Mrs. Madison and leaned over her shoulder to look. "You always side with the boys. How do you know it isn't the little husband who has run away?"

"It's Dock who stays at home," Mother Madison pointed out placidly. "Dana who goes away—"

Whiffles, looking about, suddenly asserted in loud agreement, "It's the little wife that's gone."

This was his day, he saw. He not only had his father's wonderful beetles for his own. For once he had even Mark and Matt stopped. They stood now, pressed against the other arm of their grandmother's chair, peering into the box, awed, even covetous.

"But she'll come back," Whiffles assured them all, more confidently still.

"Like fun!" said Matt scornfully.

"Twirp jelly," said Mark.

Reading in their mother's eyes that their next step would be homeward, they compromised. "How's she going to know her husband's shut up in an old case in this room?" Mark demanded.

Whiffles thought fast. "Mam'selle can put the little husband just where the door opens. He can see her then, can't he? He can tell her where to come—"

He stopped. Matt and Mark had made no sound, but their square jaws, stretched in derisive leers at such childishness, were more than vocal. In their opinion Whiffles was a sap, always running off after bugs, ready to drop anything to listen to that old violin across the road or to make sure Mademoiselle was all right.

But as they looked about their derision changed to disgust. Every adult in the room obviously thought Whiffles was sweet. Beneath their breaths they exchanged the same low, expressive sound.

Whiffles saw, heard, was enraged. "She will come back," he shouted. "Mummy always does."

"Of course she will, Whiffles," Mademoiselle assured him hastily. "See, I'll put Mr. Black Beetle right here where the case opens."

Dana, watching, listening, with mingled emotions, turned in relief as Ellen entered the room.

"Mary Bixby is here to see you, Mrs. Coyne."

Mary was there. She had followed close on Ellen's heels and now stood behind her, staring down at the beetles in the gilded box.

At best she was not an attractive girl with her tall, large-boned figure and dark, heavy features. Black braids wound round her head and thick black brows above black eyes, red and swollen now, gave her an appearance of maturity and determination beyond her years.

Perhaps it was self-consciousness, Daphne thought, that made the girl keep her head down and her hands behind her. Perhaps—as Mother Madison suspected—the child was merely trying to hide that not only her eyes but her whole face was swollen and discolored from weeping. Obviously Mary wished no sympathy from anyone, and Mother Madison's and Daphne's friendly words died on their lips.

Dana, rising, surprised in the swollen eyes an expression that suggested an intensely disappointed, if not frightened, child. She said quickly. "We won't try to talk in this bedlam, Mary. Come into my sitting room. Mother, you and Daphne will collect the family for luncheon here, won't you?" Without waiting for a reply she led the girl away.

In her sitting room she dropped into a low chair, her back to the light. Mary seated herself stiffly on the edge of another, facing her, then twisted sidewise, blinking in the strong sunshine. Here there was silence save for the click of a gardener's shears somewhere.

"You and I are alike in one thing, Mary, aren't we?" Dana began. "We don't like to talk about our troubles. Suppose we say nothing of what has happened—just talk about you and your future. Bowen says you have an aunt in California. Also that you'd like to study shorthand. I hope you'll let me—"

Mary's gesture was abrupt, almost angry. "I—I thought when I came I had something—worth a lot of money—you'd buy. Then I wouldn't need your help. I don't want it."

Dana smiled. "What made you change your mind?"

Awkwardly the girl moved to take something from her sweater pocket with her left hand. After a moment she brought her right hand into view from beneath a fold of her skirt. The hand was swollen, too, and discolored; the fingers, swollen and stiff.

With them she finally produced a handkerchief, tightly knotted about some small object. Before she tried to open it she placed the palm of her hand against her lips, sucked at it unself-consciously, as a small child does to a cut.

"Dad found this—in the woods—a long time ago." She spoke in phrases as she tugged at the knots. "He said he was going to—to keep it—for you. That you'd be glad—one day—to pay well for it. But now—why, it's nothing but a toy! Whiffles already has a lot of them. Ouch!"

She jerked her hand away, began vigorously to suck a finger. "It's got a point like a needle. That's the second or third time—"

For the space of a breath Dana sat motionless. Then she leaned forward, and, slipping her hand under the packet, picked it up. "Let me open it—with scissors."

She took a pair from the drawer of the small table beside her as she spoke. "You'll find iodine in the cabinet in my bathroom, Mary." As the girl started to protest she ordered curtly, "Use it, or at least wash your hand well. And take one of my handkerchiefs in the drawer of my dressing table. This one will never be the same again."

When after a moment's hesitation Mary obeyed, Dana cut the handkerchief open. Inside lay the missing beetle from the gilded box.

19

Wednesday Noon, July 30

Its gold was dull and tarnished; in parts, black. The shining black wings were dulled too. One hung, bent and twisted, from the body. But it was unmistakably the missing beetle.

Her eyes veiled, Dana looked at it until Mary returned to stand beside her, looking down, too, at the battered insect. "This does mean a great deal to me, Mary," she said then. "Once it belonged to Fretz Dreier, Whiffles' father. Of course it belongs to Whiffles now."

As she spoke she lifted the beetle in the handkerchief to place it in the table drawer. Mary's hand went out in protest, drew back as the drawer closed sharply.

"It doesn't belong to Whiffles—yet, Mrs. Coyne."

"There is no question of ownership, Mary," Dana told her coldly. "Your father, in my employ, found the beetle on my property. He did wrong not to bring it to me immediately."

Repressing her anger at the girl's rudeness and obstinacy, she looked up, smiling, to say, "Sit down, Mary, do. We'll say no more about this beetle to anyone. Anyone. I don't want Whiffles to hear of it until I learn whether or not it can be restored."

Mary's flushed face flushed more hotly still. She sat down awkwardly, after a moment began to rub her right hand and arm.

"And I don't want you disappointed either, Mary," Dana went on as she watched the child's discomfiture. "I won't—can't—buy the beetle from you since it already belongs to me. But I'm grateful to you for returning it. So you can accept my offer to send you—"

"But I don't want to go. I won't go." Tears shone suddenly in Mary's feverish eyes, echoed in her thickening voice. "I'm going to stay right here. In Hanotak, I mean. I'm going to find out what's happened to my father."

"And what—do you plan to do?"

"I don't know. But I don't want your money. Can't you see that?"

Mary's voice rose hysterically. "You've never taken any interest in me before. Why do you now? Something's wrong. I know it is. My father didn't run away. Why, just Monday morning he talked about staying on in the gatehouse for years and years. When I said perhaps he couldn't, that it depended on you, he said I'd see. And that very day. He went to meet you, Mrs. Coyne. And he never came back."

Something in Dana's silence stopped the rush of words short.

"Yes? Go on, Mary."

"He never came back." Mary was uneasy but shrill. "And now you want me to go to California. I don't think it's kindness. I think you want me to go away. I think you know where my father is—why he went. He's doing something for you. And you're paying him well to do it."

Dana's answer was to turn and press the bell behind her.

"Don't say any more, Mary, until Mother comes. You know her, trust her. Let her advise you." When Ellen opened the door she said, "Ask my mother to come here at once, will you?"

She sat silent then while Mary, her face half hidden, continued with increasing vigor to rub her hand and arm.

When Mother Madison entered Dana rose to draw another chair forward.

"Mary and I need your help, Mother. I've offered to send her to California, pay for a business course she wants to take. But she doubts my motives. Perhaps rightly. After all, she's seen very little of me."

She smiled as the girl tried to protest. "Now she suspects I've sent her father away—on some secret, well-paid mission. That I want her out of the way for some nefarious purpose of my own."

"Dana, you aren't serious. Mary wouldn't—"

"I am, Mother, and Mary would."

Disturbed, the older woman turned. "But, my child, you can't think that, surely."

Uncomfortable, confused, Mary tried to explain. "I—I didn't mean what I said to sound like—like Mrs. Coyne makes it. I mean—I can't seem to say what I think. It's not my father's doing something for Mrs. Coyne I mind. It—it's that while he's doing it she's not raising a finger to stop all this talk. That he's a bad man. That he's run away."

Mother Madison rose and, bending over Mary, laid a hand against her forehead. "No wonder you're talking so wildly, child. You're burning up with fever. And look at your arm! Is that poison ivy?"

"Maybe." Mary looked at her swollen arm with dulled eyes. "I couldn't stay in the house yesterday. I went all through the woods. I thought he might be there—might have had an accident. I couldn't find him." Again tears blinded her.

"You're coming home with me," Mother Madison declared. "And I'm putting you to bed until that arm is well again. You've rubbed and scratched it until you're perfectly miserable. And now you're trying to take out your discomfort on my daughter. That's all it is, Dana. The child's sick."

She placed an arm about Mary, lifted her to her feet. "When you're well again you'll understand that Mrs. Coyne—all of us—only want to help you."

As Mary's chin set stubbornly she said more sharply, "You know as well as we all do, Mary, that your father has done nothing in return for the money my daughter has paid him for two years. Do you think now she'd pay him well to do something else for her?"

"But something's happened." Miserably the child leaned against Mother Madison's broad shoulder, buried her face. "And no one believes that. Nobody'll help me—"

"We'll all help you. Come now. We won't talk any more and we'll forget all you've said."

Mary didn't lift her head. "Oh, I've been so unhappy and frightened. Waiting. Being afraid. I wish I was dead. I do. I do. I wish I was dead."

"Hush, child." Anxiously Mother Madison tried to lead the girl toward the door. "Tears won't do poison ivy any good. Wait till we have you well."

Mary straightened, wiping her eyes with Dana's handkerchief. "I'm all right now, Mrs. Madison. And I'll go home. Please, I'd rather."

When protests were futile Dana offered, "I'll send Ellen with her. She'll take you home, Mary, stay with you. And I'll come over this afternoon to see how you are."

With obvious relief Mary let Ellen lead her way.

"I wish Dock hadn't had to take that Denise child into New York for an operation this morning," Mother Madison worried as she watched them go. "Mary looks like a very sick girl to me."

Dana smiled understandingly at her mother. "There are other doctors, you know."

"Only old Dr. Herndon now. The war has taken everyone else around here except Dock. That's why he's so overworked, poor boy." She sighed and turned back toward the corridor door. "I'll ask Daphne when she expects him home."

Dana stood a moment looking after her. Then as the racing feet of the incessantly hungry twins echoed in the corridor she lifted the beetle in its handkerchief from the drawer and hurried into her bedroom.

20

Wednesday Afternoon, July 30

In the midst of luncheon, served on the east terrace, Carl Evoans was announced.

"Bring him out here, Doris," Coyne directed the maid. Rising, he moved to the portable bar. "I'll just mix him the highball I didn't offer him the other day."

"Bide your time," Dad Madison advised. "He may be coming to say he's found Bixby. If he has he shouldn't be encouraged."

"Why does he always choose such inconvenient hours?" Dana sighed.

The agent's surprise at finding them round a luncheon table at half-past two revealed he had thought his choice of hours a timely one. He refused coffee, settled for the drink, and took the chair placed for him beside Dad Madison.

"This is luck," he commented, looking about the table. "All here but Dr. Madison. I need your help."

"No luck otherwise, I take it?" Dad asked.

"Not a sign of Bixby anywhere. And that's significant, take my word for it. For one reason or another it appears that every man, woman, and child for miles around knows him. When anyone as easily identified as that has not been seen since Monday, it usually means just one thing."

"You think he's still on this property," Coyne deduced.

"Must be. Possibly even in his own house. I want to see it and his daughter again later. But first I'd like your ideas about any likely fox holes—"

"This dry, hot weather he might hide out almost anywhere in the woods," Dad told him promptly. "Except for a root cellar and a tool shed, we haven't any outbuildings on these farms now. And Pete, my handy man, was in both of them yesterday. If he'd seen any sign of Bix he'd have been pleased to say so. He hates the fellow."

"What about the pump house?" Daphne reminded him.

"That's out," Coyne declared with a brief, unrevealing smile for his wife. "Too close to this house. And Dad and I spent the morning there, tinkering round."

"Since late Monday he's neither entered his own house nor left it," Evoans informed them. "We've taken good care of that. There's a possibility, of course, that somehow, between Monday noon, when he came to see Mrs. Coyne, and my arrival later, he learned he was wanted for questioning and denned up inside his own walls."

"You don't think that or you wouldn't be questioning us two days later." Coyne looked amused.

"And you wouldn't say that, Mr. Evoans," Mother Madison protested, "if you could see his daughter Mary. The poor child's made herself ill worrying and crying over his disappearance."

"You're sure it's his disappearance? Wouldn't she worry if she knew he was hiding from the FBI?" Evoans turned to Dana. "You've seen the girl recently, Mrs. Coyne?"

"This morning. And Mother is right. Mary really is very ill, though part of it is a bad case of poison ivy. I sent a maid home with her and I'm going over this afternoon to see how she is."

"Poison ivy, eh? Sounds as if she'd been out in the woods—perhaps to see her father." Evoans turned from some thought in his mind to say, "I'd like to go over with you, Mrs. Coyne. And you'll come with us, sir?" he asked Coyne. "I want to go through that house thoroughly—but unofficially. Talk to the girl, too, if she's not too ill."

Mary was too ill. Before Evoans had finished his drink and his questions Ellen telephoned. Mademoiselle brought the message to the terrace.

"She says Mary is very sick, madame. Delirious now, talking all the time about her father. Ellen's afraid to stay alone with her and thinks you should call a doctor."

Mother Madison was already on her feet. "I'll go over at once. Daphne, you call Dr. Herndon. What a pity Dock isn't here!"

"Let me go, madame," Mademoiselle urged. "I know Mary very well. She'd be more comfortable with me—"

"Certainly not, Mademoiselle. At least, not till we know what's wrong with the girl. She may have mumps or measles." Unexpectedly Coyne was the one to protest.

When Dana rose Mother Madison was firm. "No use your coming, dear. You still look tired. I can do everything necessary until Dr. Herndon comes."

"My car's at the door, Mrs. Madison," Evoans offered quickly. "I'll take you over. And Mr. Coyne."

A frightened Ellen opened the gatehouse door to them. Mother Madison hurriedly followed her upstairs while the men remained below. One glance at the girl rolling on the tumbled bed and her call brought them up, two steps at a time.

There was little they could do except to try to keep Mary on the bed and covered. Her throat as well as her face was now dark and swollen. Her right arm was so large that the skin shone with tightness and the fingers of the hand stood out like fat sausages.

Mary did not recognize them or know they were there. Eyes wide open, she looked at nothing while her thick, dry lips moved incessantly in half-intelligible words.

Ellen hovered near the bed, half crying with nervousness and alarm. "She was all right for a while. But just before I telephoned she began to swell up like that. I made hot compresses, did everything, but she only grew worse and worse."

"What's she saying?" Evoans asked. "Sounds as if she were talking about beetles."

Mother Madison listened. "Perhaps she is. At Dana's—Mrs. Coyne's—this morning she saw Mademoiselle mounting the little boy's beetle collection. Oh, there's Daphne with the doctor!"

A moment later Dr. Herndon came nearsightedly into the room, Daphne behind him. He was an old man, practically retired after almost fifty years of general practice in the valley. His eyes peered at Mary while his transparent hand fumbled for a pulse in her left wrist.

The group about the bed watched with varying degrees of anxiety and skepticism as he worked. Finally he straightened to agree with Mother Madison that Mary was suffering from a virulent case of poison ivy. But complicated, he added, with infection resulting from scratching her arm with her own fingernails.

"She's a strong young lady," he said reassuringly. "I'll give her something to bring down that fever and put her to sleep. Guess I can trust you to bind her arm, Mrs. Madison. I see Daphne's brought some of Dock's famous poison-ivy powder. By tomorrow Mary should be much better. If not, call me again."

Reassured himself when Mother Madison said she would remain as nurse, he went away. Coyne accompanied him to his car, returned, shaking his head.

"I don't have much faith in that old hoy," he declared. "He still thinks poison ivy's a minor affliction. But I've seen strong men almost die of it in the bush."

"That poisoning angle—with the fingernails—doesn't sound good to me, either," Evoans commented. "Too bad Dock's out of reach."

"I could telephone him," Daphne suggested. "Perhaps he could get away."

"Come on," Coyne urged. "The phone's in the hall downstairs."

He paced about while she jiggled the bar in an impatient attempt to reach Central. "Why, this phone's dead!" she exclaimed. "I can't hear anything at all."

"Can't be. Ellen used it." He took the receiver from her. "Let me try." But he was no more successful in getting a connection.

Daphne turned for the door. "I'll go home, call him on our phone."

"Mind if I look around?" Evoans asked from the stairs as she disappeared.

"Go ahead," Coyne told him absently. He moved around the lower floor himself, then strolled outside. He was examining the telephone inlet to the house when Daphne came running back.

"Our phone's dead too," she announced breathlessly. "It's no use to try yours or Dad's. We're all on the same wire. Perhaps Mr. Evoans can call Dock from Hanotak."

Coyne listened, looking about. "How about that house down the road?" he demanded. "You stay here and keep Evoans here until I come back."

"Hedrick's?" Across Daphne's face fled an odd glance. "No. We—we don't go there."

"No? Well, I do. When a sick girl is concerned. What's Dock's number?"

A moment more and he was striding down the road.

21

Wednesday Afternoon, July 30

As he turned into Hedrick's private road and followed it to the house Coyne looked appreciatively from side to side. For a short distance inside the entrance the woods had been allowed to remain in their natural state, but beyond they were cleared and groomed to form a park.

Maples, oaks, elms, dogwood, hickory, firs—he identified one fine specimen after another as he strode along. Similar trees stood in the Madison woods. This winter he'd start clearing them out. Observing, planning, he progressed steadily until the closed gates at the turn of the drive brought him to an abrupt halt.

Impatiently he found and rang the bell at one side. Impatiently, when no one materialized immediately to answer it, he moved about. Once he stopped, his eyes on the sanded road. When at length an old Norwegian gardener in a faded blue smock, shears in hand, appeared, he was idly scuffing a toe over footprints there, made by small Peruvian sandals.

The old man's protest that he could go no farther he thrust aside. "I want to use your telephone," he stated curtly. "Even Hedrick can hardly object to that. Our own phones are dead, and I must reach a doctor at once."

The gardener looked him up and down, hesitated, yielded. "Come this way, sir," he said, unlocking the gate.

Coyne followed him quickly along the drive to the side entrance of a gray stone house. But not so quickly that his eyes missed a foot of the smooth, practically undisturbed sand spread over it. The Norwegian opened the door, indicated a telephone on a small table in a foyer from which stairs led up to a gallery. "I'll wait outside, sir. Will you leave by this door, please?"

Nodding, Coyne stepped in and lifted the receiver. But minutes passed before he could reach the hospital to which Dock had taken the Denise child, minutes more before his call was put through to Dock. While he waited he studied with interest the hand-woven Norwegian rugs and hangings, the water colors of characteristic Norwegian scenes, each framed uniquely in hand-wrought silver.

Once he was conscious of movement somewhere above him, but at that moment he heard Dock's voice and concentrated on giving his message.

"Damn!" Dock exclaimed when he heard. "A really bang-up case of ivy poisoning's just what I've been waiting for. But less than half an hour ago this operation was postponed, and I must stay to see the boy through it. Luckily I've got my car. I'll be there as soon as I can. In the meantime, I wouldn't worry. Mary's a husky youngster, and you can count on Mother."

As he replaced the receiver Coyne was aware for the first time of the tall fair man descending the stairs. For a space the two men remained motionless, appraising one another.

They offered a striking study in contrast and similarity if anyone had been there to see. Hedrick gained no advantage from his height and youth over the older, stockier Coyne. Coyne gained nothing from his greater maturity and practical experience over the violinist. But Hedrick was the first to move and speak.

"My name is—I am Hedrick," he said as he came forward. He smiled but did not offer his hand. "You are Carter Coyne? Pardon. I could not avoid overhearing a few words of your conversation. Someone is ill?"

"The daughter of the superintendent—the former superintendent—of Madison Farms. She's managed to give herself a bad case of poison ivy."

"Oh." The intensity of the question in Hedrick's eyes vanished. "This is the season, I believe, for such afflictions."

"Thanks for allowing me to use your phone. Ours chose this moment to die on us." Coyne turned to the door, and Hedrick moved ahead of him to open it.

"You'll feel free to come again if necessary? I'll tell my caretaker to admit you." Something of Hedrick's reserve melted. "You see, I live a very unsocial life here—see no one, go nowhere. My work—requires it."

"No one?" Coyne repeated, then smiled and looked about from the doorstep. "Well, if one must live in seclusion, this is an ideal place to do it. I borrowed several ideas for—for Madison Farms—as I came along. But isn't it possible to carry seclusion too far? I believe you're an old friend of my wife's. She'd be delighted to know you are here and to see you."

"Thank you." Hedrick's tone became reserved once more. "I live here, Mr. Coyne, as Hedrick—a Norwegian violinist. Hedrick, unfortunately, has no American—ties."

He stepped down. "If you will excuse me, I'll instruct Ole." With a formality that amused Coyne he bowed and moved quickly across the drive to meet the old man in the blue smock emerging from the trees. Or perhaps his amusement was for the rounded prints Hedrick's sandals were making on the white sand.

22

Wednesday Night, July 30

Midnight had just passed when Coyne, drowsing uncomfortably on the steps of the gatehouse, roused to recognize Dock Madison coming up the path from the road.

"Left my car at the main highway and walked up," Dock greeted him. "Didn't want Daphne to hear it and come tumbling out at this hour. Lord! I thought I'd never get here."

"Thank God you're here now." Coyne already was leading him into the house, hurrying him to the stairs.

At their top Dock stepped into a small bathroom. "Tell me as I scrub up. That Mary moaning now? Surely poison ivy couldn't—"

"No comment," Coyne told him curtly.

Dock shot a sharp glance at him, scrubbed furiously, dried his hands as he strode to the door of the bedroom at the back of the house.

Unlike the average young girl's room, this one lacked any sign of the trifles usually dotting walls and tables. An old-fashioned bureau, a double bed, a single straight chair, and a small table beside the bed on which stood an alarm clock, all made of shiny pine, formed its total furnishings. Obviously Mary considered it merely as a place to sleep.

She was not sleeping now. Neither was she conscious of Mother Madison, anxious-eyed and weary, trying futilely to keep her on the pillows.

Dock suppressed an exclamation, flung aside his towel. Silently, swiftly, he set to work but shortly straightened, holding Mary's right hand, palm upward in his own. When he had studied it closely his gaze turned on his mother.

She moved stiff lips in a scarcely audible murmur. "I—I saw that too."

Anger and concern darkened Dock's face. "This is no case of poison ivy. Though I can understand why you thought it was, Mother. It's poison all right, but I'd have to have an analysis to say what. And there's no time—or need—for that now. Mary's dying. She may live till morning. Not longer."

His mother gazed at him in stunned dismay. Then as fear or horror moved in her eyes he asked quickly, "What is it? If you know anything, tell me."

"This morning—I was remembering." Her tired voice faltered. She looked at Coyne. "When Mary came to see Dana she looked feverish, sick. But we all thought she was overwrought, had been weeping for her father. She talked so wildly Dana sent for me, and when I saw her arm—I thought of poison ivy. It's so common now."

"That isn't what you started to tell me, is it?"

"It may not have meant anything. We didn't think it did, of course. But she said over and over she wished she were dead. You don't think she—" Mother Madison stopped as tears filled her eyes. "Oh, how stupid, how wickedly stupid we were! Thinking of poison ivy when the poor child—"

"Don't blame yourself, Mother. Herndon agreed with you, remember."

Dock stooped to lift the girl back onto her pillows, cover her gently. Then he walked to the window, stood with his back to the room, looking out. When he turned, his face was hard, decisive. He spoke to Coyne.

"You said Evoans was here this afternoon? Knows about this?" He nodded toward the bed. "Then how does this idea strike you? I haven't been here. You haven't seen me, talked with me—except by phone. Wait." He put up a restraining hand as his mother started to protest. "There's nothing I can do—anyone can do—for Mary. If there were I wouldn't suggest this."

"Go on," Coyne told him.

"I'll return to New York. Remain there till morning. Then I'll come back—I can make it by ten, I think. I'll get hold of Evoans, bring him out with me, explain on the way. This may tie up with Bixby's disappearance, may not. If it does, he may want to keep it quiet—"

Dock paused, but no one commented. "In the meantime, call Herndon. No, you can't, can you? I'll call him somewhere along the road, explain that I can't get out, ask him to come over. He'll stay—give you a certificate of death. Whether or not we use it depends on what Evoans wants to do."

"You think Bixby is dead too? This way?" Coyne asked.

"Dock!" Mother Madison turned to her son before he could speak. "You don't think Bixby has been back—did this!"

"I don't know what to think and I'm not going to try. The child's suffering horribly but doesn't know it much. Herndon has her pretty well doped, and she's growing weaker. I'll take specimens for analysis and be on my way. That is, if you agree with me."

"I vote yes," Coyne said.

"Yes, yes. Go, dear," his mother urged. "Let the poor child die in peace. Perhaps this is best for her too. She hasn't had much of a life."

"Lord, I hope I'm not stepping too far off the line," Dock murmured to Coyne when he was ready to leave. "But I can't think of a better solution at the moment."

He was gone, leaving Mother Madison and Coyne beside the bed of the dying girl, each wrapped in his own thoughts. Once Coyne roused to take Mary's hand, study again the two tiny discolored spots in its palm, and return it gently to its place under the covers.

23

Thursday Morning, July 31

Shortly after ten the next morning, Evoans, Coyne, Dock Madison, and his mother gathered soberly in the living room of the gatehouse. Mary was dead. Dr. Herndon, as Dock had foreseen, had placed his signature on a certificate of death and gone his way. The bit of paper lay on the table now, and all their eyes were on it.

"I know how you people feel," Evoans said, breaking the silence. "But don't take the responsibility for this girl's death so completely on your own shoulders. I'm as responsible as anyone, if it comes to that. I thought it a strange case of poison ivy, but I'm no expert, and Doc Herndon's idea that Mary had infected herself put me off. You all did what you could. It was just bad luck that Dock Madison had to be in New York and Herndon the only man available."

He turned to Dock. "And that was fast thinking on your part, young fellow. I didn't put much weight on Mary's saying she wished she were dead. Might be, of course. We've got to consider suicide as a possibility. But there are other angles. And this"—he nodded toward the certificate—"gives us a chance to work unhampered."

"Maybe," Dock conceded darkly. "But there's going to be plenty of talk. You can count on that."

"Maybe," Evoans agreed, shrugged. "You'll do all you can to determine the cause of the girl's death? Good. Then until further notice we'll let the certificate ride. For one reason, because it's possible Bixby himself is dead. That whoever is responsible for that is responsible here. For another, because it's equally possible he's still alive. Alive and not far away. From what I've heard, he wasn't too good to his daughter. He may have considered her existence a threat to his own in some way. Perhaps Mary knew where he is hiding. Perhaps knew more about his activities than was good for her. Or stumbled onto something after he left."

The detective talked slowly, speculatively, with frequent pauses to give them time to comment, but no one spoke. With a sigh he picked up his hat, concluded: "I suggest you make arrangements for Mary's burial as soon as possible. Carry on as usual. Since your phones are out of order, I'll stop in Hanotak on my way and send an ambulance out."

When he had gone Dock lifted his mother to her feet, started her homeward. "You're to go to bed and stay there until tomorrow. Keep Dad at home, too, and don't tell him any more than necessary. C. C. and I will take care of everything here. And no regrets, Mother. You did just what you thought was right and did it splendidly."

He walked with her to the door, stood watching her out of sight. From a living-room window Coyne watched, too, until Dock returned, threw himself into a chair.

"God! I wish I knew whether I'm a hypocrite or a patriot," he muttered angrily. "If the truth were told, my quick thinking, as Evoans called it, was one part for him, two for us. It's time these Farms had a break!"

Coyne cocked an alert eyebrow. "Meaning?"

"In two words—that you have a spectacular wife and I have a spectacular sister." Dock looked at his big hands, back and front, then lifted his eyes to gaze straight into Coyne's. "Plain, simple, everyday things just don't happen to her or to anyone connected with her."

"We've time for more than two words, Dock."

The younger man smiled at him briefly. "I'm glad you're here, C. C., and that I can talk to you frankly. It's all very well for Evoans to suggest we carry on as usual. But there's plenty of talk going round now about Bixby. There'll be more when word of Mary's death gets out."

"Talk's cheap! What of it?"

"This. For every word about Bixby and Mary there'll be a dozen about Dana. You see, when she's away we all live pretty humdrum and normal lives. But when she returns lightning strikes. As if she were some agent that attracted it, diverted it to others. Daphne and I can take the talk. It's Mother and Dad who suffer—"

"You think Dana—"

"Lord, no! She's harmless—if a bit high-powered for these parts. Bix disappeared, but, as you know yourself, Dana hadn't even seen him. Mary dies. Well, according to Mother, the girl was sick when she came to see Dana yesterday. And that was the first time Dana had set eyes on her in two years."

"Then what are you trying to say?"

"Trying's the right word. It's a long story. I could begin almost anywhere—from the time Dana was old enough to talk. But I guess the last ten years are enough. Dana started them off with a flaming romance with Blake Amery that lit up the whole valley. It ended in fiasco, and that was a sensation too. At the same time—" Dock paused abruptly, added, "Skip it," and went on in another tone:

"Dad scraped the bottom of the barrel to send her to Cornell while the valley recovered. I was married to Daphne then. The twins were due, and all this didn't do my efforts to build up a practice any good either."

He looked up again to smile an amendment. "But it made me a darned good doctor. Had to be—to survive. I think I cured anyone who had the temerity to send for me by sheer will power. I had to stay here because Dad and Mother couldn't remain alone."

Coyne nodded. "Go on."

"Dana came back the next year, married to Fretz Dreier. A grand fellow and a really fine scientist. Life at Madison Farms took a turn for the better until—three summers later—chasing a butterfly, he met a rattlesnake."

"I know about that."

"That fall Dana went to New York, returned a few months later married to the same Blake Amery who—I'll skip that too. He was pretty much of a snake himself, but he met a better one. And died—alone in the woods. That sent Dana off by plane to South America. Now she's back"—Dock lifted tired, harried eyes to smile warmly at Coyne—"married to the grandest guy in the world. Her marriages to Dreier and Amery shook the valley up considerably. Dad and Mother too. But this one! Well, your name isn't exactly hidden under a bushel, sir, as I'm sure you know. Thanks to you, Madison Farms was in a fair way to live down its purple reputation—"

"When Bixby disappears and Mary dies," Coyne completed for him. "Haven't you forgotten something? Hedrick?"

He chuckled in his throat at Dock's startled expression. "Met him yesterday afternoon. And liked him. Rather an exotic type—to a man like me—but much more real and well balanced than some geniuses I've known."

"I did pass up that particular dynamite," Dock admitted. "Or perhaps I was waiting for the detonation."

He crushed out his cigarette with more care than necessary. Coyne, watching, suggested shrewdly, "And now you think Madison Farms should be allowed to return to its humdrum and normal life?"

Dock laughed in relief. "You're too fast for me, C. C. I was planning a graceful way to ask if your wide interests didn't require your presence elsewhere."

"I never keep a dog and bark myself," Coyne informed him dryly. "My interests are in good hands."

"They would be! Well, then, here it is. As I said, Daphne and I can take the talk and all that goes with it. And that pretty well means social ostracism. For one reason, because Dana's second father-in-law—Senator Amery—and the whole Amery clan maintain what amounts to a dictatorship over the valley. He's retired now and can give his complete attention to it. For another, after Dreier's and Amery's deaths, people far and wide got the impression that this place is infested with dangerous reptiles.

"No one comes here. You must have noticed that. But let that go. It's Mother and Dad I'm concerned about. It's time they had some peace and pleasure and satisfaction in their lives. They were here first. And they're entitled to live out their lives in the one place that means home to them."

Coyne rose to place a hand on Dock's shoulder. "Thanks, son. It wasn't easy for you to say all that, I know. I've not been unaware of the lightning. As a matter of fact, I like it. If one knows how to handle it, and I think I do, it can be both beautiful and useful."

He dropped his hand, moved round the room as he talked slowly. "Dana and I are staying right here. For one reason, as you like to say, because the only way to solve a situation is to see it through to the end. You don't heal your patients by bottling up a disease in the body but by getting it out of their systems. And we—you and I—are going to see this through so that Dad and Mother can have the life they want and deserve."

At the sound of a heavy car stopping before the house he concluded hastily, "That's all. And here's the ambulance. You run along and get some sleep. I can—"

He stopped, swung round to face the hall. The telephone was ringing.

24
Thursday Morning, July 31

"Darling," Dana's throaty voice asked the moment Coyne spoke into the receiver. "What's the matter? Mademoiselle has just told me you didn't come home all night!"

He waited for the echoing footsteps of Dock and the two men with a stretcher to grow quiet above his head. "Mary is dead," he said then.

"Dead! Mary? Of poison ivy!"

"Later. Right now I want you to send Ellen or someone here to stay in the house. Ana Bowen to take me into Hanotak. And to know how you happen to be telephoning."

"But of course I phoned. The moment Mademoiselle told me. She's right here beside me with Whiffles and Bunny. They missed you first thing—"

"Don't you know our phone—all the phones on this wire—have been out of commission since yesterday afternoon?"

A moment of deep silence, then Dana confessed remorsefully, "It's my fault, darling. I—we—Whiffles and Dock's boys and I—played telephone company after you left yesterday. We have a switchboard here that controls all the phones. Blake Amery had it installed, but we never use it now—"

"The details later. What happened to the phones?"

"I don't know, really. Mademoiselle can tell you. I imagine one of the children disconnected something. I didn't notice. Mademoiselle discovered it this morning. Put back whatever was out of place. Do you want to talk to her? Why, she's gone!"

"No matter. Later. Just send Ellen and Bowen at once, will you?"

"Of course. But, darling, wait. Your voice sounds so tired, so dry. It's awful about Mary, of course. Poor child! I'm so sorry. But—"

"Later," Coyne told her again. "Not now."

He returned the receiver to its cradle, walked to the door to gaze out over the quiet lawns. Another clear blue day. And warm. Going to be hot. As Dock and the ambulance men came slowly down the stairs with their burden he stepped aside without speaking.

When the ambulance had driven away Dock turned at the gates to look back questioningly. Coyne shook his head. Dock hesitated, then walked over to his own car, got into it, and drove homeward.

Coyne was still standing in the doorway when Bowen, at the wheel of the big closed car, swung round the drive and stopped. Sober-faced, the chauffeur jumped out, hurried to the steps.

"Ellen will be here in a few minutes, Mr. Coyne. Is there anything I can do?"

Coyne walked out to the steps to look down at him gravely. "You knew Mary Bixby?"

"A little, sir." The young man's face flushed. "I—I met her Monday afternoon while I was taking a ramble around the grounds. When you didn't need me in the evening I came back. She was all alone here, worrying about her father."

"How did she strike you? As a well-balanced youngster or emotional? Able to stand up to trouble or go down under it?"

Bowen twirled his cap thoughtfully. "Maybe a little too well balanced, sir. I—I liked her, you understand. A fellow appreciates a sensible girl—occasionally. And she was a swell cook."

A twinkle glimmered in Coyne's eyes, went out. "But—"

"But I guess she was something like her father, sir. From what I've heard of him. Kind of set in her ways. I mean she'd got an idea about her father and wouldn't listen to reason."

"Reason?"

"Well, it isn't uncommon for a man to go off like her father did. Bixby evidently had been up to something. Even she admitted—Tuesday—that he'd been very different lately. So it was more—more stubbornness than anything else, as I saw it, for her not to consider the idea of his going away for his own good."

Coyne nodded, changed the subject. "Did you notice—did she say anything about not feeling well, about this poison ivy?"

"No, not on Monday, sir. But Tuesday morning when I came over to see if she'd heard anything from her father she was all—all sort of red, sir. Nervous. Didn't want to talk. Didn't even ask me in. I didn't think she was so much sick as flustered, as if I'd arrived at a moment when she didn't want me to see someone or something, But later, when I came over with a message from Mrs. Coyne, she looked pretty miserable."

"Unhappy or ill?"

"Maybe both, and excited and a little frightened too. She couldn't keep still and seemed to have something on her mind. When I told her Mrs. Coyne wanted to see her she said at first she wouldn't go. That Mrs. Coyne could come here! Then she said she didn't need help—wouldn't take it."

"You think she believed or knew her father was alive?"

"Believed it, anyway. I don't think she knew it."

"She seems to have talked with you pretty freely."

"Because she was lonely, I guess. She didn't seem to have any friends her own age around here. But the two Mrs. Madisons, she said, had been very kind. Asked her to stay with them until—"

"Say anything about where her father might have gone and why?" Coyne interrupted. "We're interested, you know, in finding him."

"Yes sir." Bowen smiled. "That FBI agent asked me a few questions. And also to keep my eye out for Bixby. That's one reason why I developed a sort of—of friendship—with Mary." Embarrassed, he paused.

"Ever arranged for a funeral, Bowen?" Coyne asked then, "I had intended to go into Hanotak myself, but if you could go for me—"

"If you've got the doctor's certificate, certainly, sir."

"Just like that, eh?" Coyne's eyes twinkled again, pleased.

"Yes sir. You see, my father is superintendent of the Willmore estate in Pennsylvania. It's a pretty big place, and I helped him with all sorts of things until—"

"Until?"

Bowen hesitated, looked up frankly. "Till I had so many ideas myself about how things should be done there wasn't room for two of us. That's how I happened to be free when you needed a chauffeur. I jumped at the job because I thought it would give me a chance to look around this valley, maybe see a place—"

Coyne's smile brought a flush to the young man's face. He laughed a little himself, "I guess you see what I'm leading up to, sir. Only I was going to wait—"

"So you think you could manage Madison Farms, do you? Well, why not? At least we can give the idea a trial for the rest of the summer. If we're both right we can make a permanent arrangement later. That suit you?"

"Yes *sir!*" Bowen's whole face glowed. "Now if you'll give me the certificate, Mr. Coyne—"

25

Thursday Noon, July 31

Coyne remained on the veranda, smilingly following the car Bowen was sending straight and swift as an arrow down the road to the main highway. In his mind he could see the telegram that shortly would be speeding, also, on its way to Bowen's father.

His smile vanished, however, before an Ellen, stiff with resentment. "You don't come gladly, do you?" he asked gravely.

"No sir, I don't," the maid told him flatly. "I'm just new here, sir. I didn't know this girl. And didn't like what I saw of her. There's plenty of people round more responsible for her than I am. But I'm the one that had to take care of her while she was raving crazy out of her head. And now I'm the one to stay in this house alone again—"

"Raving crazy? That's a new expression to me."

"That's what she was, sir. Plain raving crazy. She talked sixteen to the dozen every minute. At first I thought she was talking in her sleep. Then she began to roll around, crazy, too. Such talk for a young girl! Only seventeen, sir."

Coyne made no attempt to restrain her resentment. In fact, when she came to a pause he said, "You and I appear to be in the same boat, Ellen."

When her surprise changed to understanding he added, "As just a couple of strange new brooms here, let's see what we can do to clean up the situation. If you can remember what Mary said I may be able to discover something that will help us—about relatives, her father—"

Mollified, Ellen became loquacious. "Nothing she said would help anyone much, Mr. Coyne. She talked a lot about people here—Dr. Madison's wife and Mrs. Coyne especially. She—she didn't have much use for them. Jealousy, I suppose. And she talked about her father—didn't seem to have much love for him, either. But she said she knew he hadn't run away. There was too much reason, she said, for him to stay right here, sir."

Ellen paused to qualify her statement. "She didn't say things clear, like that. That was what I made out of her talk from her going over and over everything so often. But after a while she talked mostly about beetles. Over and over, until I was almost crazy with hearing it, she'd say, 'It wasn't a beetle; it was a bite.'"

"'It wasn't a beetle, it was a bite,'" Coyne repeated. "You're sure that's right?"

"Just that, sir, over and over."

"Odd phrase. But, then, delirium is an odd thing. Any idea what she meant by it?"

"No sir, except that those beetles of Whiffles—and those bright ones in the gold box—were all over the floor when Mary followed me into the living room to see Mrs. Coyne. Probably because they were one of the last things she saw, they made an impression on her. So she mixed them up in her wild talk."

"Sounds reasonable, and thanks, Ellen. I can understand that you didn't have an easy time. And I don't think, after all, there's any reason why you should stay here today if you don't like the idea. The house is empty now, might as well be locked up. I'll do that."

He overrode the maid's halfhearted protests, watched her hurry away, relief in every step. Then slowly he entered the house, shut and locked the door.

Methodically, beginning in the ample basement, he began to search. The basement gave evidence that Bixby had found numerous ways to make additional sums of money for himself. Crates and baskets and well-built bins testified to the substantial business he did in selling fruit from the orchards, vegetables from the fields. At one side, baled paper, bottles, assorted and sorted, farm implements, even shoes, books, toys, suggested a miniature secondhand store.

The little attic, reached by a ladder and a trap door, told of other activities. In comparison with the starkness of the furnishings of the house itself, contents of trunks and boxes revealed constant pilfering from Dana's closed home, possibly in anticipation of the more comfortable days he saw ahead. Soft blankets, linens for bedroom and dining-room use, silverware, a small rug or two, gold and silver trifles—all were carefully folded or wrapped away, some dusted with insect-killing crystals.

He looked at each object carefully, returned it to its place, and closed each trunk or box. Then he attacked the single shelf. There in box after box were evening wraps, gowns, lingerie, gloves, hose.

Standing on a box, Coyne went through them quickly and stepped down. If Bixby had run away, he thought as he surveyed the room, his departure had been precipitate and unplanned. Even on a few days' or hours' notice the man would have made sure nothing remained in this attic to betray his studied thieving.

As deliberately Coyne searched the bedroom floor, then the main floor. Nothing anywhere suggested that the house had served as a home to its occupants. Merely as a place to eat and sleep and take shelter. Only once did he pause, his face darkening. Tucked into the back of Mary's dresser were some small, cheap pieces of lace for table use, a blue glass vase, some bright picture calendars, treasures the child also had put away for some brighter day.

The room he saved until the last, originally intended for a small dining room, had served Bixby as an office. An old roll-top desk, with a portable typewriter on a small table beside it, a lamp, and a straight chair made up its equipment.

Pigeonholes and drawers of the desk were crowded to overflowing with a miscellany of old letters concerning materials, bills, faded packages of seeds, match packets, balls of string, wire, and other debris.

Patiently Coyne went through each one, sorting, reading. Nothing. No bank- or checkbook. Not even an account book of expenditures and receipts. Not a letter or a note that revealed the address of friend or relative. Only a pad of delft-blue paper and some excellent stationery engraved with the name, Madison Farms, in one drawer suggested that Bixby ever sent anything out. And no carbons of the weekly reports both Dad and Dock had described had been preserved, either.

As he emptied each drawer Coyne pulled it out to tip the residue of burned matches, nails, dust, empty typewriter-ribbon boxes into the wastebasket. The desk searched, he was about to rise, when fragments of adhesive tape about one small square tin box moved him to retrieve it.

With a tentative finger he turned back the raw edge of a grayed and stained fragment of adhesive that had once sealed it but now showed signs of being recently cut. The raw edges were almost white against the gray of the outer side. He shook the box again and smiled at himself. Still empty. About to drop it again in the basket, he stopped and pried open the close-fitting lid.

For a long moment he gazed at the contents. A bed of soft cotton. A bed of soft cotton that registered the outline of the small object that had lain there for some time. At one end of the imprint was a tiny dark stain.

What the stain meant, if anything, he did not know. But for the third time in two days he recognized an imprint when he saw it.

26

Thursday Afternoon, July 31

The little tin box in his pocket, Coyne locked the gatehouse, started wearily homeward in the hot noon sun. But as he neared the house he hastened his steps, smiling. A sight to smile at did lie ahead.

Whiffles had drawn his shining red truck, a duplicate of the great commercial trucks on the highway, even to a length of chain dangling on the ground behind, to the step of the east terrace. Now he was prancing before it like a high-spirited steed.

Bunny, a blob of upended pink, supported on two sturdy legs, was bent almost double behind it, prepared to push. And in the wagon, arranging herself to fit, sat Dana, slender and cool in a green play suit. With a ribbon about her blond curls, her knees under her chin, she looked little older or larger than Whiffles.

Coyne, approaching unnoticed, stopped to demand sternly, "Does Mademoiselle know you youngsters are out alone?"

Dana turned round, laughing, reached for his extended hand, and jumped out. "We were just about to set out in search of you, darling. You've been gone altogether too long."

Bunny corrected her croquet-wicket posture to remind her mother. "First we go for cookies. This day Chang makes them." As she spoke she sidled round the truck.

Coyne's eyes twinkled with delight as he watched her take advantage of Whiffles' back to climb into the wagon and seat herself firmly.

"Off you go then," he advised. "Tell Chang I'm on his cooky list now."

Turning with Dana to the terrace, he dropped into a chair with a sigh of relief. "In the meantime, I could use a long, cold drink." As Dana pressed the bell he added, "Everything's taken care of, dandelion. Bowen's doing all right. He telephoned from Hanotak just before I left the gatehouse. He's arranged for a small private funeral from a chapel there. Tomorrow afternoon—early. Just the family."

Dana, seating herself near him, studied her slim legs. "It can't be helped, I suppose. I always dread—going to funerals."

"No, it can't be helped. We must all go. I couldn't find the name of a single relative or friend anywhere in that house. You don't know of any?"

"An aunt—out West somewhere. I don't know her name. Mademoiselle may. I'll ask her later. She's so furious now she's given herself a headache."

"Furious? Why?"

Dana shrugged. "Because of that beetle case of Whiffles, for one thing. You must admire it loudly the first time you step into the living room when he's around. It's above the fireplace and really looks better than I expected. Thanks to the gold beetles."

"Mademoiselle doesn't approve of its being there?"

"Not entirely. Though the trouble really is over the missing beetle. Whiffles—Bunny, too—are both sure it will return. They call it Mrs. Black Beetle. Whiffles made her place Mr. Black Beetle just at the bottom of the case where the door opens. That way Mr. Black Beetle can see and open the door for his wife when she comes back."

Coyne's tired face relaxed in a grin. "What's wrong with that arrangement?"

"Mademoiselle feels the gold beetles are too valuable to be exposed like that. She wants the case locked. Whiffles and Bunny won't hear of that. And I supported them."

His amusement changed subtlety. He looked around the floor, straightened to smile at her. "Hear that dull thud? That was a dozen years or so rolling off my back. You and your offspring, trifle, are good medicine for this ageing frame. I'd forgotten there was a world where the domestic affairs of a pair of beetles, dead or alive, could bring on an emotional crisis in a household. How is the headache? Serious, I hope."

Dana laughed with him. "It will be. Migraine. Thank heaven Mademoiselle only gets them once or twice a year. They take days—"

"She takes her responsibilities too heavily."

"Oh, the beetle case is only the minor reason. She's chiefly angry because no one told her Mary was so ill. Because she was not permitted to go over, do anything for the girl. While I was away she and Mary seem to have become friends, but how was I to know that? When you telephoned this morning that Mary was dead she flew out of my room—has been weeping and striking ever since. I've been playing nursemaid."

"A career with a future." Coyne twinkled at her. He looked up as Ellen appeared with highballs and sandwiches. "Good for you, Ellen."

"I thought you'd need them, sir, when I saw you coming home." The maid hesitated, gave him a brief but friendly smile, and returned to the house.

"Nice girl, Ellen." Coyne attacked the sandwiches with enthusiasm. "Capable, too. So's Bowen. I'm moving him into the gatehouse as soon as we can refurnish it decently."

When Dana's swinging sandaled foot stopped in mid-air he explained, "Going to give him a chance to replace Bixby."

Dana set down her drink, untasted. "You're going to what?"

"I've had a lot of time to think about you and me and this place and everyone on it since I saw you yesterday, trinket." His eyes met hers for a moment, went on to gaze at the baking lawns and trees.

"This is my home, too, now, don't forget. And where my name is concerned I'm sensitive. I'm buying these farms from you, as of yesterday or today."

She placed both sandals firmly on the floor before she said, "I don't understand, Carter. Does it matter in whose name the Farms stand?"

"It does, indeed. To me. To your father, to Dock. Thanks to Dock and Evoans, we've escaped—perhaps—a very unfortunate situation. I want to be in a position where I can be sure nothing of the kind can happen again."

"I still don't understand."

"Don't you? Don't you realize that if you'd understood your responsibility for your employees you'd never have left a child of seventeen alone in that gatehouse for three days?"

"Mary? But—"

"And when she did come to you—sick, unhappy—that you should never have sent her home with a strange maid, to lie for hours without a doctor's care? Oh, I know you thought she was suffering from poison ivy."

"She wasn't?"

"Poison, yes. Not ivy."

Dana sat back, shocked, incredulous. "You mean she—Mary told Mother and me she wished she were dead. But of course we never dreamed such a child—"

"From now on I don't want you to have to think about anything but being Mrs. Carter Coyne. We both need the rest and change a few weeks can give us. Let's say between now and Labor Day. In that time I want to try out Bowen as superintendent and to work out plans with Dad and Dock to get these Farms organized for production. There's a war on, my dear, a detail, it's difficult to remember in this quiet pocket of the world."

He quirked an eyebrow at her. "It seems I'm making quite a speech. And I might as well finish it. I want a man here—as butler, major-domo, whatever you want to call him—to be responsible for the house and servants. I have that man. Jackson's out West, but I'll wire him to come on. With him and Bowen, if he works out, and I'm betting he will, we'll both be free—"

"But, Carter! Darling, listen!" Dana sat forward to place a hand on his knee. "I won't—can't—sell my Farms to you. I've spent more than effort and money on them. And they mean much more than land and houses and gardens to me. I'd as soon sell Whiffles."

Her urgency vanished, and she lightened her voice at unmistakable signals of determination in his face. "Neither is really necessary, is it? Nothing is mine in that sense any more. Everything's ours. Have Bowen if you think he's a good man; Jackson, too. And do what you think best with the Farms."

Coyne shook his head. "I didn't expect you to say yes at this moment. But for both our sakes, the Farms must be in my name."

She shook her head decisively but smiled too. "Let me talk a little now," she said, picking up her drink and sitting back. "I've been thinking too, darling. And your ideas about Bowen and Jackson fit in with mine that we'd be foolish to tie ourselves down in this pocket, as you call it, too tightly. We can live anywhere—New York, California, Canada, Florida—"

"And Whiffles? Bunny? You plan to move them from one corner of the hemisphere to the other?"

"We don't have to move them. This would remain our home, of course. It's a wonderful place for children. And Mother and Dad adore having them there when I'm away. With Mademoiselle they're no trouble. And Dock's here, too, to take care of every scratch and bump. We could come here to see them, have them with us when—"

"It's convenient?"

"Naturally."

"And Mother and Dad Madison? Dock and Daphne?"

"They'd really be happier if we weren't here all the time. You must see that. They each have ten acres. That's all they really need or want. And if we leave a good superintendent here they wouldn't have a thing to worry about."

Coyne drained his glass, set it down firmly before he rose.

"You are selling the Farms to me, my dear. My lawyer is arriving from New York in the morning. Between now and then you can decide on your price and reach your own lawyer if you like."

"And if I refuse?"

"You won't refuse. Call the sale—tentative, temporary, what you will. But as long as you bear my name you must permit me to make the decisions, handle any affairs that affect it. Of course, as we agreed, if one day you tell me you have found a younger man you wish to marry, the Farms will return to you."

She tried unsuccessfully to turn her eyes from the question in his. "But why must I *sell* them?" she protested finally and, when his impenetrable gaze still remained fixed, added, "And why are you so sure I will?"

"Because the time when you can play at being a wife, a mother, the owner and administrator of these Farms is ended. You must either meet your responsibilities or turn them over to others."

"My responsibilities!"

"You can no longer run away from them. That has been your method, hasn't it?"

Dana sipped her drink slowly while her mind raced back through their conversation, trying to trace his purpose through it. "You think I may want to run away again?" she asked him unexpectedly.

His glance approved her directness. "I think there's going to be trouble over Mary's death. Bixby's disappearance too, probably. I'm losing no sleep over him, but Mary is a different story. In your mother's words, we were all 'wickedly stupid' about her. In mine, criminally negligent."

Dana's intent gaze lightened. "You mean talk? Why should I want to run away from that? There isn't much more anyone can say about me."

Before he could answer she tossed up her hands, smiling at him in apparent capitulation. "Have it your own way, darling. And if you must know, I would like to run away. But with my husband. I bring him here and what happens? My family, my lands, even the fish in my river, seduce him."

At his quick, pleased laugh she jumped up to, say lightly but definitely, "Since I can't hold my susceptible husband, I'll keep my Farms."

"And your husband—I hope." He was amused but not swayed. He rose, too, as he saw Ellen had arrived to announce luncheon. "Give me ten minutes, will you?"

He turned to the doors but paused in them to say, "By the way, the woods are safe for little rabbits now. I've seen the chap who's been making free with them. Go where you will. He's harmless."

27

Thursday Afternoon, July 31

Dana remained as he had left her, head tilted back, the smile with which she had acknowledged his announcement still painted on her lips. But her mind, pricked again and again during their conversation with doubts and uneasiness, was not similarly idle.

Her husband, she knew, was mistaken in believing her the trinket, trifle, toy, orchid he enjoyed to call her. Was she also mistaken in her estimate of him?

Beneath that calm, indulgent, even affectionate surface he offered her, she had early recognized an adamant will and purpose. But she had also early recognized her own power to please, amuse, and interest him to achieve her own ends. Now, when perhaps for the first time in her life she was forced to consider herself in relation to another, she found her confidence shaken.

Carter, she realized, actually did regard her as a minor moon revolving about himself as sun. A small diverting moon whose direction, course, and speed of movement he himself would regulate. The realization first rocked her, then swept her with anger and resentment.

For a moment she did not know that she was listening to him speaking to her brother on the telephone.

"Dock? . . . You awake? . . . Just back from a round of calls?" His laugh at some reply of Dock's roused her.

"Well, can you keep your eyes open for an hour or so longer? . . . Good. I'll be over right after luncheon. Before we talk with Evoans again I want you to see something I found in the gatehouse."

As she heard the receiver settle back in its cradle Dana drew in her breath, sucking in her lower lip. Then quickly, as if waking from an unpleasant dream, she shook her head and entered the house.

In the living room she met Mademoiselle, the gilded box in her hands. "What're you doing with that?" she demanded sharply.

The governess turned a wan face toward her but did not look at her as she answered. "I'm taking it to Mr. Coyne, madame. He sent Ellen to ask me to bring it to him."

And little more than an hour later Coyne, the box under his arm, arrived at the door of Dock's screened porch. His surprise as he saw Dad Madison there also, expectantly waiting, brought the old man to his feet.

"Hi, Dad!" Coyne said quickly. "Don't go—unless you want to. Three heads may be better than two when all I've got is a hunch."

Dock swept a small table clear of magazines and cap pistols. He looked tired and worried.

"Daphne's gone to the day camp to pick up the boys. And Bertha's in the woods somewhere, hunting blueberries. Guess this is as good a place as any to see what you've found."

"First, look at this." Placing the beetle box on the table, Coyne turned back the domed top.

"But that's Fretz Dreier's," Dad exclaimed. "I saw it yesterday. In your living room when Whiffles showed me the gold beetles mounted with his own. Don't know as I approve of that. Fretz didn't think more of his two eyes than he did of those little gold insects. And one's lost already, Mother says. She's pretty upset about it."

"You didn't find that box in the gatehouse," was Dock's comment.

"No. I just want you to look at it first. The beetles are gone, of course, but each one has left a clear imprint on the velvet."

Puzzled, Dad and Dock obediently peered into the box with its eight empty pockets, each with its outline marked as if drawn in white against the graying velvet. Puzzled still, they looked up at Coyne.

"Now see what you think of this." He took the little tin typewriter-ribbon box from one of his own pockets, opened it, and placed it on the table also. "This is what I found in Bixby's desk. Shoved back in a drawer under old letters and bills."

Dock pursed his lips in a silent whistle as he looked from the imprint on the cotton to the duplicates on the velvet. "So one of the beetles is missing. Daphne did mention that. And you found this in the gatehouse? Looks as if it weren't missing—very far."

Coyne nodded. "That's what I thought."

"What's your hunch?"

"I'd like to ask some questions first. For one, how did Blake Amery die?"

"I told you. Rattlesnake bite."

"You saw him yourself, Dock?"

"Well, yes. At the funeral, that is. Daphne and the boys and I were on a holiday at the time. Cruising around New England in the car—it was new then. A telegram caught us at Keene, New Hampshire. We got back the morning of the funeral."

"Then you weren't the doctor called when he was found?"

"No. Bartlett. He's with the Army Medical Corps now. Good man."

"Bartlett was convinced snakebite killed Amery?"

"Yes." Dock's tone became wary. "Specifically, rattlesnake bite. He had an analysis made, of course."

"Rattlesnake venom is even more specific. You agreed with him?"

"Well—I made no examination myself. But the lab report"—Dock hesitated—"I accepted that."

"What are you driving at, C. C.?" Dad interrupted. "Sure Blake died of rattler bite. I saw the two little points on his arm where the fangs—"

"You saw them too, Dock?" Coyne asked.

Dock didn't answer. His thoughts obviously were elsewhere.

After a moment Coyne asked, "You thinking of the two small discolored spots in Mary's right palm?"

No answer.

"Look like the marks on Amery's arm?" Coyne persisted.

No answer.

He nodded sagely. "So that's why you and Mother Madison looked at one another last night as if you'd seen time collapse! I'd a hunch then you'd both met those spots before." His tone changed. "How many people have you seen die or even bitten by rattlers, Dock?"

Suddenly alert, the young doctor came out of his thoughts. "In spite of the reputation of Madison Farms, just one. Fretz Dreier. What's on your mind, C. C.?"

"I've seen plenty of bites. Rattler, moccasin, copperhead, scorpion, viper—almost any kind you can mention. None of them looked like the marks on Mary's hand. It occurred to me that if those spots resembled the ones on Amery's arm you might have been mistaken about the way he died."

Dock started. "That's a pretty serious charge to make."

"I'm making no charges. Just asking questions. And that look I caught between you and Mother Madison over Mary's hand isn't all that started me thinking. I learned something this morning from Ellen. She listened to Mary's ravings, you know."

Both Dock and Dad were seated now, leaning forward over the little table, their eyes pinned on Coyne's face. But neither spoke.

"Out of all Ellen could remember, one sentence said something to me. 'It wasn't a beetle; it was a bite.' That say anything to you?"

"Not to me," Dad assured him promptly. "Mary was a strange girl in many ways. Sometimes I couldn't make sense out of what she said in her right mind."

Dock was scowling thoughtfully. "I'd hate to place too much importance on such a sentence. What does it suggest to you?"

"Plenty." Coyne's, voice was grim. "To me it says that Mary's muddled mind was trying to explain what happened to the child. Trying to say that a beetle that wasn't a beetle could bite. Did bite her."

His listeners stared at him. Dad, bewildered. Dock, skeptical.

"And that suggests to me," Coyne went on with slow emphasis, "that one of Fretz Dreier's gold beetles—though not a beetle—could bite. Did bite."

Dad smiled faintly. "Who's raving now?"

Dock didn't smile. "The missing beetle, you mean? Assume for a moment you're right. Then what?"

"This is where you—and Dad—come in. All I have is this." Coyne lifted his smallish left hand to check off his findings on his fingers. "One, Mary's odd sentence. Two, the discolored spots on the palm of her right hand. Three, the way you looked at your mother, Dock, when you saw them. Four, the imprints of the beetles in Dreier's box and of an identical beetle in this little tin box. Five, my sketchy information—a little clearer now—as to how Amery died. Putting them all together, I came out with an idea—"

"I hope you're wrong," Dad interjected.

"—an idea that maybe Amery didn't die of snakebite. That maybe he died of beetle bite. The kind of bite that killed Mary."

Dad stirred uneasily. "Looks to me as if you're getting ready to set off a lot of trouble, C. C. Blake Amery's dead. Mary's dead. What's the use of going out of your way to find bridges to cross?"

Coyne smiled reassuringly. "We'll come to that later, Dad."

"Bixby!" Dock exclaimed. "You think Bixby's at the bottom of this?"

"Might be," Coyne agreed. "Bixby obviously has always had an eye out for any opportunity that would put extra money in his pocket. Blake Amery, if not rich, as I understand it, was at least rich enough to represent a source of income to a man like Bixby."

He saw the look that flashed between Dock and Dad but made no comment. "Now, this is where I need help. Would it have been possible for Bixby to uncover something in Amery's life on which to base blackmail? Or do you know of anything that Bixby did that might have turned Amery against him? I'm just fumbling around. But is there anything that might have moved Bixby—out of fear or desire for revenge—to kill Amery?"

Dock rose suddenly to move about. "You certainly have something there, C. C. Amery loathed Bixby. Did everything he could to force Dana to get rid of him. In fact, he even had a switchboard installed in their house that controlled all the phones—just so that he could keep an ear open on Bix. Dad and I killed the switchboard idea, and Dana refused to dismiss him. Chiefly because she never neglected an opportunity to make Amery's life miserable."

"And Bix loathed and, I think, was afraid of Amery too," Dad contributed reluctantly. "And it was Bix who found his body. Perhaps the reason he was able to find it—if there's anything to your hunch, C. C.—was because he knew where to look. But where does the missing beetle fit into that?"

"Just two more questions," Coyne said. "First, assume Bix had some reason to wish Amery dead. Second, remember the immediate acceptance of Dreier's death by snakebite. Given a reason for murder and an unquestioned method of death, wasn't Bix the sort of man to adopt snakebite as an ideal means of disposing of Amery?"

"Good God!" Again Dock was on his feet. "Look here, C. C. You're not questioning Dreier's death too!"

28

Thursday Afternoon, July 31

"Sit down, Dock. No, at the moment anyway, I'm not questioning Dreier's death. I'm assuming Bixby wasn't too bright. I never saw the man, but, from what I've heard, I know his type. Imitative but never creative."

Dock seated himself again, and Dad released the tight grip he had taken on his chair arms.

"Sorry to upset you, Dad," Coyne said then. "Just think of this as a fishing expedition. Haven't caught anything yet. May not. All right? Now—let's assume that Bixby wanted to dispose of Amery with rattlesnake bite. How would he simulate it? He'd seen the marks of fangs on Dreier, just as you all had. Been impressed with them—if that was the first death of the kind around here. He had—or thought he had, anyway—to inject the venom with something that would make duplicate marks. Logical, so far?"

"We're listening," Dock told him noncommittally.

"Just before I came over here I examined one of the gold beetles in Whiffles' case. It—they all have two fine, sharply pointed antennae. I didn't experiment, of course, but it looked to me as if their bodies could hold a minute quantity of liquid, eject it through those feelers. And the evidence of this little box proves that Bixby had opportunity to see and appropriate one of them."

"Aren't you skipping a step?" Dock interrupted. "First, he had to get the venom."

Coyne sat silent for a moment, his eyes on the opened baroque box. "Let's assume he had it—or knew how to get it," he said as he tilted the cover and closed the box.

Impressed by the silence around him, he glanced up. Dad and Dock were looking steadily but with blank eyes at one another. His gaze went over them speculatively.

"My next question brings me to Mary," he went on quietly. "Assuming Bixby killed Amery with venom ejected through the antennae of the missing beetle, what would he do with it afterward? If you'll visit the gatehouse with me later you'll see he wasn't the man to destroy or throw anything away. Especially anything as valuable as that beetle. Or, having succeeded with it once, he may have thought to keep it for further reference. Anyway, he hid it in what to him was a place both accessible and safe. Who would think to suspect an old typewriter-ribbon box among a mass of forgotten bills and letters in his desk?"

He paused.

Dock said, "Speaking of Mary—"

"All right. This is my guess as to what happened to Mary. Her father disappeared sometime Monday afternoon. Mary wouldn't believe he ran away. She searched the house for something, anything, to give her a clue as to where he'd gone and why. As I did, she came on the typewriter-ribbon box. It was sealed with adhesive tape. She cut and pulled it off, found the missing beetle.

"Curious, if nothing more, she took it in her hand. Perhaps she did not notice the two sharp antennae. Perhaps some sound startled her and she closed her hand to hide it. In any case, she pressed the antennae into the palm of her hand. Rattlesnake venom still contained in the beetle entered a vein—"

"Assuming, also," Dock inserted, "that the venom was still in condition to be ejected and to poison."

"Naturally. Though remember, the box was sealed airtight. Some kind of poison was working in her yesterday when she came to see Dana."

Dock sat forward, interested. "Why not try out Evoans' idea that Bix may still be alive and near by? Perhaps he himself opened the box—took the beetle when he skipped out Monday. Perhaps he learned, among other things, that Mary is telling strange chauffeurs, anyone who will listen, that her father expected to have a great deal of money soon. Perhaps he returns—perhaps his return is the reason Mary insists so steadily he has not run away. Perhaps to silence her, insure his own safety, Bix uses the beetle a second time."

As Dock and Coyne sat back, considering their theories, Dad rose stiffly to his feet to look down at them with dulled and fatigued eyes.

"You two have raised some dangerous questions. And you may have caught the tail of a logical theory. I could fill in some background to support it. But I'm not going to. Why raise the past? Pile new troubles on old ones? I wish you could see your way, C. C., to forget all this. It's all based on ifs, anyway. Isn't any point that I can see to justify mentioning this to Evoans."

"We've not finished, Dad. At least I'm not." Coyne rose too. "I'm going to suggest that Dock compare the analysis he receives on Mary with the one made on Amery's death. My guess is he'll find them the same. That's concrete, isn't it?"

"If they're the same, yes."

"And I'm going to suggest that a third analysis be made to prove that the venom came from the missing beetle—"

"First produce it," Dock advised.

"We don't need the beetle at the moment." Coyne picked up the little tin box, balanced it on his palm. "We can have this imprint on the cotton photographed or sketched, can't we? That would prove that for some time the missing beetle remained in Bixby's own desk. And—"

"But wouldn't prove the beetle contained venom," Dock pointed out. "And your whole argument rests on that, C. C."

"Look again." Coyne placed a finger above the minute stain on the cotton. "We can have that spot analyzed. If it proves to be, as I suspect, rattlesnake venom, then we can talk to Evoans."

"But why?" Dad protested again. "Mary's dead. Will be buried tomorrow. Bixby's gone. There'll be talk, of course. But if you let it alone it will die down."

He moved slowly round to Coyne, placed a hand on his arm. "We're glad you're here, C. C. Don't mistake me on that. But you haven't been here a week yet. We've lived here—Mother and I—all our lives. Seems as if now we ought to have the right to say something about what's to be done and not done. Why should you—"

"Why?" Coyne's deep eyes were warm with sympathy and understanding for the old man's distress. "Because I'm determined to wipe out what Dock calls the purple reputation of Madison Farms. Don't you see there'll always be misunderstanding, trouble, until the responsibility for what has happened here is placed where it belongs? In less than a week Madison Farms has come to mean a lot to me. It's my home too. And I've ideas—many of them your ideas, Dad—about ways we three can make this place sit up and sing."

Dock rose abruptly, troubled eyes on his father. "You're right, of course, C. C. The way to get rid of trouble is to face it down. But Dad's right too. And he and Mother have borne the brunt of all that's happened. Will happen. If he wants to forget this, why not?"

He turned to look at the boxes on the table. "Evoans could never tumble to all this on his own."

"No." Coyne shook his head. "I can't. I'm involved in this, and so is Dana. I'm buying Madison Farms from her tomorrow."

29

Thursday Afternoon, July 31

In the surprise and satisfaction his listeners found in Coyne's announcement no one heard swift, light footsteps in the living room, whose wide windows opened on the screen porch. Dana, rising from the chair in which she had listened comfortably to all they said, sped through the house and out a side entrance.

Her feet were winged. She could have danced, sung, laughed aloud in an exultation of freedom and relief. Her mind whirled with words and phrases from her husband's theory of Bixby and the beetle. And they all added up to one thing!

She had only to settle down at Madison Farms, take root there, show reluctance to leave even for a day in New York. She had only to become the Mrs. Carter Coyne her husband wanted her to be, and no ghost could ever rise to confront her.

What a fool she had been to suggest that they live elsewhere! But perhaps not. To accept Carter's preference to remain on the Farms, yield gracefully and completely to his judgment would please him. She could see herself doing it, hear that single deep note in his throat he always uttered when he was pleased.

Even if her funny, heavy husband couldn't prove his case against Bixby she was safe. Safe so long as she remained on Madison Farms as his wife. Even if questions—suspicions—rose against her, she was safe.

Nothing could be proved against her so long as Coyne's tenacious finger pointed straight at Bixby's door. Reasonable doubt—those were the words. With Carter to fight for her, there would always be reasonable doubt.

She flung up her arms joyously. How glorious the day—the sky so radiantly blue, a garden itself with small white clouds opening against it like flowers. How sweet the scent of petunias, of the blossom-hung bushes, of the pines drowsing in the hot sun.

A shout of triumph, a shriek of anguish pierced her self-absorption. Looking ahead, she laughed softly to herself. The children, she saw, were about to embark on an hour of croquet. Whiffles was dancing down the outside stairway to the play porch, flourishing a mallet aloft. Apparently Bunny considered that mallet her particular right, for like an enraged huntress she followed, her mouth wide open. As Dana watched, Mademoiselle—headache or no headache—appeared above, her arms full of wickets, stakes, and balls.

Immediately, at some word from her, Whiffles surrendered the mallet to Bunny, ran up the steps again to assist in carrying down the set. Bunny tossed the mallet over the railing to the ground and turned back also. Thank God for Mademoiselle, thorns, emotions, headaches, and all!

She herself had no desire to endure a croquet match. Leaving the walk, she crossed the narrow sward of grass on the left to the apple orchards. Aimlessly, happily, she wandered among the laden trees until she reached the path that led to the picnic grounds.

Happily, singing to herself, she followed it. But when she stood in the entrance to the grounds the song stopped. The charm of the place took her breath—so green, so quiet and cool, so golden in the afternoon light sifting through the branches of the trees.

She must come here every day. Arrange picnics. Have swings set up for the children. In the stillness, made deeper by the hum of insects, she moved toward the picnic benches. Belatedly became aware of the quiet figure leaning against the shelf of the fireplace, watching her.

Rick! In the moment she recognized him he came to meet her. Her heart was singing, but she remained motionless, studying him.

How tall he was, how well defined, how decisively he moved. The nine years that had made him Hedrick had disciplined him harshly but given him hardness and distinction. Why hadn't she seen that before?

"At last you come, my Dana," he greeted her softly, stopping a pace or two from her. "Could you feel me willing you to come?"

Her answer was to throw herself into his arms, eager to feel their young hard strength about her.

His eyes lighted coldly, though they were dark, too, and intense. His lips crushed against hers, and he held her closer as she abandoned herself to his kiss. When she lay in his arms, clinging, shaken, powerless to move, he picked her up, carried her to the broad seat near the fireplace. Roughly he placed her on it, stood before her.

"You little fool! Now tell me you're Mrs. Carter Coyne! You're mine. Have always been. Will always be."

She lifted eyes as dark and ardent as his own. How young and strong he was. How marvelous as he stood there, his blond head framed in green, his eyes ablaze.

When he did not move or speak she stirred uncertainly. Why was he regarding her so steadily, his eyes unfathomable now, reminiscent, curiously, of Carter's.

"Rick! Oh, to have you come—today! I've longed for you. Wanted you so. Always—"

"Always? Hardly, my Dana. Shall we say from Tuesday night?" He smiled enigmatically. "Oh, I don't doubt you want me—now. Body, mind, soul—and reputation—you want me now."

"Yes. I want you now."

"A pity!"

She started. Bewildered, mistrusting her ears, she gazed at him, repeating the two icy words in her mind. As if he had struck her, she dropped her hand, shrank back against the seat. Before the cool, cynical smile in his eyes her own fell.

"What is it?" she asked, her voice thin, uncertain, even, in her own ears. "You're changed. Different. Cruel."

"In nine years one learns." He laughed. "Also in nine seconds!"

A small flame of jealousy kindled in her eyes as she looked at him. "Women have taught you?"

"Perhaps."

"But you've changed since Monday—Tuesday—" She was silent, remembering. "Nine seconds? Now, you mean? You learned?"

"That your kiss for Rick and for Hedrick are two different kisses."

Two small spots of color flamed in her cheeks. She sprang up. "You think it's because I know you're Hedrick I want you—now?"

He laughed. "I know it's because I'm Hedrick. Hedrick! The great violinist. The artiste!" Bitterly he mocked her. "Now I am no longer Rick, the fiddler, you melt in my arms. Invite me—"

The two small flames vanished from her cheeks. Uncertainly she gazed at him.

"So? You are silent? You do not now tell me you are Mrs. Carter Coyne. Because I am Hedrick you stand there like a little—peasant. If I open my arms you will come to them like a ripe plum."

He paused. "See! You have not even the spirit to speak. To walk away. You are afraid I might not come after you. You are terrified—I can see it in your eyes—that I have learned—"

"That you do not love me?"

"That I do not want you."

Too shaken to stand longer, she sank down on the seat. "Yes, I am terrified," she confessed after a moment. "If that is what you want me to be, Rick. In all my life I've leaned on you, knowing you were across the road, across the ocean. Now I don't know. Now I'm terrified."

"Good." He smiled. "Now we can talk. And you can quiet I your fear. I still want you. More, I'm going to have you."

His smile vanished as he watched the change in her face. "I have learned from you, my Dana. As you learned from the Senator. To be cold, ruthless—cruel, as you say—to take what I want."

Reassured, she leaned forward and, seizing his hands, drew herself up before him. "Don't tease me, frighten me, any more. I want you, Rick. And Hedrick. Both of you."

He loosed her grip, stepped back. "I don't doubt your love, my Dana. But love across the road or across the ocean! Pretty words in the woods! Let us talk no more of love until you can join me."

Again her gaze became uncertain, frightened. She turned to look across the low wall to the orchards and the broad roof of her home visible above the trees. Was she the woman who had just passed so joyously down Dahlia Walk, wandered in those orchards? As she stood there, feeling Rick's nearness, her own longing for him, cold again touched her, ran in lightning waves over her body.

She could never leave Madison Farms, never leave Carter Coyne now! Yet Rick would accept her no other way. It was no longer hers to choose between Rick and Carter. That had been done for her. Slowly she turned, her face pinched and white, to face him.

"It's too late, Rick."

"Why?"

"Carter—"

"He would not agree to a divorce? Then leave him!"

"He would agree. I can't ask for one."

"Why?"

"Stop asking me why. I can't."

"Because of your children?" Mockery edged his voice. "No? Surely not because of your husband, your family."

"No. No. But it's impossible."

"Why?"

She turned again to gaze into the green tangle of woods. They appeared like prison walls now, with sunlight sifting through dark bars. He watched her, unmoved.

"Because of Bixby?"

She whirled back. Stood rigid, staring. "You—know? Saw?" Almost imperceptibly he nodded.

The tip of her small tongue moved to moisten her lips. "What are you going to do?"

Again that odd smile for her. "That's better. You ask now what *I* am going to do. But it is not I; it is you who must choose."

As she continued to gaze at him, mesmerized, he said coolly, "You are going to ask your Carter Coyne—today—for a divorce. Or you can leave him. Either way—if it is ever necessary—I will swear you killed Bixby in self-defense. That I saw and heard him threaten you but could not reach you in time." He waited.

"Or—?" Her lips formed the word she could not speak.

"Or I shall tell what I did see—and hear. Twice an agent of the FBI has called at my home. To ask Ole and my houseboys about Bixby, the possibility that he may he hiding on my property. I was not—at home—either time. Tomorrow he comes again. After Mary Bixby's funeral. I shall be at home."

"You're trying to frighten me, force me. You wouldn't!"

"No?"

"Because you love me."

"As you love me." At his smile she shrank back again. "Yet you could throw my violin in the fire, tell me you would not marry a poor fiddler. And you could marry a Fretz Dreier, a Blake Amery, now a Carter Coyne—loving me. Because they had a name, money—"

"But, Rick, you understood then. You knew that to live on this farm—with nothing—would have killed our marriage. That's why you went away." She tried to smile at him. "Became Hedrick."

"That fool—who pours his heart into the strings of a violin for money and applause!" Rick stopped, suddenly threw back his head, and laughed. Laughter without mirth.

"Stop that!" she cried. "Stop it."

He stopped. "I laughed at myself. I—who damned you for the same thing! We are two of a kind, my Dana. We belong together."

"It's too late, I tell you!"

He stood over her, cold again, implacable.

"The choice is yours to make, my Dana."

Before she could speak he turned away. As she took a step to follow he reached the woods path. She made no further effort to stop him, but before he was lost to sight among the trees she knew what her choice would be.

30

Thursday Night, July 31

When for the second time Dana sped up the private road to Rick's home she found the gate at the turn of the road open. Beyond, on the terrace beside the pool, she saw Rick himself waiting for her. Waiting was the right word. He did not descend to meet her.

"You knew I'd come," she accused when she stood beside him.

"I knew you'd come."

"You know my decision?"

He nodded.

Her lips tightened, then she laughed. "You do understand me, don't you? Aren't you pleased—and to see me?"

She bit her lip then. How could she be so naive! What new power had Rick to transform her into this self-conscious, uncertain-peasant?

"Safety comes first with my Dana," he told her. "Pleased? Naturally. Interested, too, to see what devices have occurred to you—to have your cake and eat it."

She started, But he had turned to indicate two lounge chairs on the grass near the pool. "Shall we sit here?"

Silent, nonplussed, she followed, sank into a chair, and leaned back. Let Rick speak now. She was tired, terribly tired. The hours since he had left her in the picnic grounds had been crowded with thinking, planning, working.

"You have not talked with your husband?"

"No. No—not yet."

"Yet you have come—"

"Rick," she implored, "don't be so cold—so far away. I need you."

"Tell me, then."

"No, not now. Not ever, I hope. But I can't do everything alone. I do choose you. Not because of safety. But I can't—talk to Carter until I've made sure of other things first."

He leaned forward suddenly, searched her face, his eyes so concentrated that she shrank from him. "What is it? What are you thinking?"

He sat back, but his eyes still held hers. "I was trying to read your thoughts, my Dana. Bixby, I can forget. Amery, too—if what Bixby hinted is true. They are better men dead. But—no—others!"

Her face grew stiff with horror. "No, no," she gasped.

"You swear it?"

"Yes. Yes, yes, yes."

"Do not tremble. It does no harm to understand these things and one another." He took her cold hand, placed it against his lips. "See, I seal them. Forever—unless you force them open. I will not—cannot—be silent another time, my Dana."

He placed her hand back in her lap, curved his lips in a faint mocking smile. "You see, I am Hedrick. I have a name and reputation, too, to—protect."

He leaned back and sat in pregnant silence for a time. At length Dana stirred. Like Mary Bixby, she drew from her sweater pocket a handkerchief, knotted about a small object. Before opening it she looked up apprehensively.

"Don't ask questions about this. And don't laugh when you see it. It's very important. Everything depends on it."

She untied the handkerchief, folded it back to reveal the missing black-winged beetle. The stains were gone now, but the gold body was still tarnished, one wing bent on a slant.

He lifted it curiously, held it to the light falling over them from trees behind their chairs. "But this is exquisite. Where did you get it? I've never seen anything like it outside a museum."

"Oh, it's valuable," she agreed indifferently. "But, Rick, it's more than that to me. I must have it restored. No—wait. It isn't simple. I—no one can take it to a jeweler. I thought you might know of someone, someway—"

He looked at her sharply, then examined the beetle again. "It's not badly damaged, really. Anyone with sufficiently delicate instruments and touch can repair it." He stopped, rose. "Wait here. Peder, one of my houseboys, does excellent work with silver. I'll talk to him."

When he had gone Dana, reassured, lay back in her chair, gazing about the grounds with fascinated eyes. What a beautiful and peaceful place Rick had made of the old cluttered farmyard. To remain with him here, peaceful, too, safe . . . She sighed. So many obstacles still remained.

She had thought of them all when she returned to her rooms from the picnic grounds. Thought of nothing else as she worked frantically to clean the stains from the little beetle, then to wrap and tie and mark gifts from South America for the Saturday-night fiesta. Thought of nothing else while her lips exchanged gay banter with Carter and the youngsters who had come to help. Carter, surprisingly, had brought in many gifts of his own to add to the confusion and anticipation. And tomorrow he and Whiffles were going into the woods to find a tree!

They wouldn't be disappointed, she promised herself. It would be the first and last fiesta they would have together. She would make it memorable.

And Carter, she thought, would not be the obstacle she had feared. He already loved Madison Farms as if he had lived there all his life. She would let him have them, bribe him, as it were. When she had carried out her plan about the missing beetle the greatest obstacle would be removed.

But if Carter had the Farms, she realized now, she could not remain here with Rick. Her parents, Dock, Carter, himself, would make that impossible. Because of the children. If she left Carter for Rick she must leave everything.

Why not? A wave of exaltation swept her. To have real love at last—a young man's love, strong, ardent. Not an old man's love like Fretz's. Not a paternal, amused affection like Carter's. She did not even think of Blake's. To be with Rick at last—what would it matter where she was? To be with Hedrick—to travel, share his fame . . .

She roused as she felt him beside her, looked up to see he had been following her thoughts.

"Good news," he said. "Peder leaped at the chance to restore the little beetle. No, don't be alarmed. He is an artist with metals." He sat down on the foot of her chair. "The restoration of this beetle is all that remains now before you can talk with your Carter Coyne?"

"I hope so," she agreed uncertainly. "But you must give me time. I'm as impatient as you are. I want you so much it frightens me, blinds me. But I want safety, too, for you as well as myself."

He nodded. "Tomorrow, then, I will not see this man from the FBI. But he will come again."

"You don't know Carter," she declared unhappily. "I can't go to him, say, 'Free me,' and expect him to say yes. I must make sure everything is—is in order, that I can answer all his questions—"

"Questions?"

"Oh, I made a terrible mistake. I should have told him I had seen you, talked with you. Now he mustn't know. He's a strange man. Kind, generous, too generous. But, underneath, deep and immovable as a rock."

"I do know. I've seen him, talked with him. And I denied, too, that I had seen you." Rick paused thoughtfully, shrugged. "I've known men like him in Europe. They have ideas, ways that are not ours, my Dana. They're inflexible, a law unto themselves. The man has principles, my Dana. And they are dangerous. God knows why he married you. Certainly he does not know you for the unprincipled little tiger you are. And you must leave him before the day comes when he does. With such a man that day cannot be distant."

She moved uneasily. "You're trying to frighten me again. He's hard, inflexible, but not—not what you say."

"You don't really see others—except as they relate to you. That others see, feel, think, are capable of acting, too, is beyond your range."

"You think Carter knows about us?" She stopped, thoughtful, also. "He knows this—that you're the man who visits Pelleas and Melisande."

"Now you're the one who's afraid of shadows. He can't know that. I haven't been there since Monday—"

"He knows the man who came there is blond. How tall he is, how he walks. What kind of sandals he wore. When he saw you he must have recognized—"

"So!" Rick rose to pace about. "That explains the impression I had that he knew me. I thought he might have heard me play somewhere. And didn't really care for me and my music." He tried to smile at her, but his face was concerned.

Dana rose, disturbed, too. "I know now why he told me today the woods are safe. Tuesday he warned me to keep out of them. Yesterday he saw you. He knows! He said that to watch me—"

"Nonsense. He is no spy. According to his own standards, he's an honorable man. But he is astute—quick to grasp implications. He doesn't need footprints, a dropped handkerchief, to tell him. He read me like a book. He can read you. That's why you must leave him—before he reads too much."

Dana was not listening. She was trying to recall Carter's words, attitudes, in the few times they had been together since they arrived at the Farms. She could not remember. But tonight at dinner he had said his holiday was nearly over. Telegrams, cables, correspondence were catching up with him. And he had gone to his rooms almost immediately to prepare for his conference with some lawyer in the morning.

Did he really intend to work? Or was that merely a ruse? Had he followed her here? Was he watching her from the shadows of the park?

Rick laughed at such fears, repeated that Coyne was not the man for such tactics. Finally he placed her back in her chair, brought out his violin.

But Dana could not relax as he played. Fears—a thousand fears—harassed her. Carter was not blind like Fretz, a fool like Blake. How could she have been so blindly foolish as not to see that for herself?

The violin's smooth tones rasped on her nerves like a file. Her one desire was to get away—return home—see Carter. No, her one desire was for Rick to take her in his arms, hold her, reassure her. Stop watching her—that odd light in his eyes—as he played. He knew she wanted his arms, his kisses, his love. He was deliberately withholding them, using her need as a weapon.

When Ole at last appeared, crossing the lawn to them, she jumped up, went to meet him. The old man inclined his head gravely but passed on to place the beetle in Rick's hand.

Rick examined it, pleased. "It is like new. Peder is an artist." Peder was indeed an artist. The tiny golden legs and feelers were exactly in place. The slanted wing fitted the body smoothly. And the gold shone under the light.

Twenty minutes later, the beetle in her pocket, Dana slipped through her French doors into her dark sitting room. But with her hand on the cord of the tall lamp just inside, she paused, startled. Someone else was there also!

"Carter?" she asked.

"No, madame. Mademoiselle." A switch clicked under the governess' hand, flooding the room with light.

31
Thursday Night, July 31

Dana's relief found release in anger. For a moment she studied the gray-faced woman standing just inside the door, noting that not only headache but some deep personal emotion had drawn deep lines about her eyes and mouth.

"It's after midnight, Mademoiselle," she pointed out icily. "What reason can you have for being here at this hour? It's not the first time today you've come when I was away."

"No, madame, it is not." The governess's voice was dry, uneven with strain. But she stood firm, her determination plain. "I came here this afternoon to talk with you—to warn you. You weren't here. Tonight I waited."

"To warn me? Aren't you taking too much responsibility—for a governess, Mademoiselle?"

"If I were only a governess, yes. But I am much more. I am almost the mother of your children, madame. I love them as if I were their mother. It's because of them—"

"Whiffles! Bunny! Something's happened?"

"No, madame. So long as I am responsible nothing will harm them."

Weariness suddenly overwhelmed Dana. "Oh, go to bed, Mademoiselle. If they're all right this is no time to come to me. Whatever you have to say can wait till morning."

The governess did not move. "We must talk tonight, madame. Now. You cannot go on like this."

Dana whirled round, amazement greater than her anger.

"Please, Mrs. Coyne, sit down, listen to me. I did not come to make you angry. Because of the children I'm trying to help you."

Unwillingly Dana did sit down. But her silence was not reassuring. She snapped open a cigarette box on the table beside her, took out a cigarette, threw it away. "Get on with it, then, please."

"You make it difficult." Mademoiselle hesitated, moved forward, and sat down in a chair to face Dana. "You do not understand your children, Mrs. Coyne. To you they are little animals—like pets. Something to play with, amuse you."

"Mademoiselle," Dana repeated mockingly, "you do not understand me. And at this hour I'm nothing—to play with. If you have something to say, say it and go."

"You have no right to leave your children to me for years, madame, permit me to love them, care for them as if they were my own—then resent my speaking when I see you harming them."

"I! Harming my own children?"

"Yes, madame. You know how you fascinate them, delight them. To them you are something lovely, amusing too. But that is not enough. They want to be with you. To have you love them, understand them, play with them as they see young Mrs. Madison do with Mark and Matt. They are not toys. They see and feel. You do not even see them every day. And they count on seeing you. On their good morning with you. You have them come one morning, not the. next They talk all day about what they will tell you when you come to say good night. How many times have you come, madame?"

"I pay you to amuse and care for the children when I'm home as well as when I'm away, Mademoiselle. If they feel any lack, the responsibility is yours." Dana moved to rise. "Good night—"

"No, madame, sit still. I have more to say. I will not stand by and see them cry themselves to sleep. See them watch you go into the woods, their hearts in their eyes to go with you."

"You will not? You are saying you wish to leave? Very well, Mademoiselle, leave. Tomorrow. Tonight, if you prefer."

The governess shook her head patiently. "You must listen to me. You have married a good man. You have a wonderful life here ahead of you for yourself and your children. And you are throwing it away. You must not—"

Dana's eyes narrowed. "I must not! Do you know any reason why I cannot live my own life as I wish to live it?"

"Yes, madame. I am the reason."

"You!"

"I, madame. You know that when Mr. Evoans asked if Bixby had come to the house at 5 p.m. to see you I said no, he had not."

"What else could you have said? He didn't come."

"I could have said—and proved—that he did not intend to come here. That his note did not read '5 p.m.' but 'five, p and m.' That he meant you to meet him at the pools, Pelleas and Melisande, at five, madame. And that you went."

"Nonsense!"

"Mr. Evoans can read for himself, madame. As you know, I have Bixby's note to you. It is proof enough."

"Of what? What are you trying to say?"

"That Bixby went to the pools at five, madame. And so did you. He never returned."

Dana slid forward quietly. Her voice was level though her lips hardly moved. "Are you threatening me? This is the second time, isn't it?"

Mademoiselle's quiet matched her own. "And the last, madame. For the sake of your children. You must not destroy their home and their love and trust in you. They have a chance now for a normal life, a good life, with a father and mother. Already they worship Mr. Coyne. You must let them have that life."

"And how am I destroying my home, Mademoiselle?"

The governess's dark, drawn eyes lifted, looked straight into hers. "That I do not need to tell you, madame. You think I do not know where you go at night, where you were tonight? Whom you meet when you enter the woods? You cannot conceal that long from Mr. Coyne."

"You intend to tell him? Is that what you're trying to say?"

"No, madame. Don't you understand? I'm not speaking for myself. I know that when the children are grown I must leave them. But I've poured my heart into them. I love them. And you are destroying what I've given my life to do for them. What Mr. Coyne can do for them—if you are not here, madame."

Dana drew in her breath slowly, did not speak.

"I am saying, madame," Mademoiselle told her softly, "that if you do not give me your word to see no more of Hedrick I will place Bixby's message in Mr. Evoans' hands."

Dana's voice was as soft. "And who is destroying my children's home now?"

"If it must be destroyed, the sooner the better. Before they know too much, suffer too much."

"You think Evoans will take the word of a hysterical woman—with a scrap of paper—against mine?"

"A scrap of paper—and other things."

Dana sprang from her chair. Unaccountably the governess smiled.

"I have no reason to regret Bixby's disappearance, Mrs. Coyne. If you follow my advice you will have nothing to fear from me." She rose slowly, moved forward, her face drawn with more than physical pain. "I know it is only because of Professor Dreier's will you have not sent me away, madame. And I will promise you this. If you will give the children the life they need I will break the will—go away of my own accord—when I am sure."

For a long moment the dark brown, almost black eyes met Dana's dark, almost purple gaze. Then the governess added softly, "Otherwise, madame, I shall tell Evoans of the message, the cane, what Mary took me to see in the gatehouse Tuesday morning—many things I have observed that would interest him. It would not be a question of my word against yours."

Dana stepped back, sat down. The governess remained silent before her, waiting.

When Dana looked up her face was smooth, half smiling. "You are saying that if I agree not to see Hedrick again you will remain silent? Is that bribery or blackmail, Mademoiselle?"

"Both, perhaps. They are the only weapons I have to use in defense of your children, madame."

"And that if I agree to follow your suggestions—your orders—you will return to me the note from Bixby you have no right to keep?"

Mademoiselle shook her head. "I will destroy it and leave here when I am sure the time is past to need it, madame. But so long as the children are happy, have a real home, I will remain silent."

Again Dana drew in her breath, sucking in her lower lip until the tips of two small white teeth showed. When she spoke her voice was quiet, almost amiable.

"Perhaps you are right, Mademoiselle. So much has happened since I returned, I hadn't realized how little I'd seen my children. I think you can be assured they will have a real home—after tomorrow."

"Tomorrow?"

"After Mary's funeral. You will permit me to be there, I hope."

The governess winced, then color flooded her face. "You place me in a false position, Mrs. Coyne. I am not a jailer. I only want—

"I know, Mademoiselle." Dana smiled with her lips again, rose. "You only want the happiness of my children. And now you have worked yourself into a state where you hardly know what you're saying. You'll make that headache worse if you talk longer. Good night."

Mademoiselle hesitated, unsatisfied, doubtful. "I have your word, madame? I—I do not wish to repeat this experience. It has been very painful to me."

"To me also. No, we will not speak of it again. You have my word."

Reluctantly, still mistrustful, but unable to penetrate the glazed courtesy Dana now offered her, the governess turned and without a word left the room,

Dana sped to the door, switched off the lights. Then, peering out, she watched the tall figure walk slowly down the dim corridor, watched the living room grow darker as Mademoiselle moved round it, turning off lamps. Shortly she appeared beside the stairs, stood a moment looking about, then, after turning off a lamp there, mounted, a dark silhouette against the one night light left burning over the mantel.

A moment later Dana stood at the foot of the stairs herself, listening until she heard a door close above. Swiftly she moved to the fireplace, after a glance about opened the door of the beetle case.

It was not difficult to remove Mr. Black Beetle, waiting there so patiently for the return of his wandering wife, to substitute instead the missing beetle and close the case.

Listening again, Dana stood with Mr. Black Beetle in her hand. Not a sound. Swiftly she moved to the stairs. In the upper corridor she paused. A dim light there, another in the playroom at the end revealed all other doors closed.

Purposefully now, she crossed the corridor to the narrower stairway leading to the attic. There, the door closed and locked behind her, she remained some time. To open Fretz's great chest, to find a logical place among all the apparatus and personal possessions Mother Madison had packed so carefully there was not the work of a moment.

Even when she found what she sought, inside the ripped lining of a hand-tooled leather box Fretz had prized, she remained looking reflectively at Mr. Black Beetle in her hand. Was she right to destroy Carter's theory of Bixby and the missing beetle? The discovery here at some future date of what would appear to be the missing beetle would do just that—irrevocably.

But she had thought it all out so clearly that afternoon as she cleaned the real missing beetle. If she left Carter she must have another line of defense. And one day—if her father or mother remembered that Bixby had been in New York on the afternoon Blake Amery wandered into the woods—Carter's theory automatically would fall apart anyway. No, she must not depend on anyone but herself.

Resolutely she stooped and slipped Mr. Black Beetle behind the ripped lining of the leather box, returned it to the chest. Then with a final glance about the shadowed attic she moved to the door, turned out the light, opened it.

With her foot on the first step to descend, she drew back. Soft slow sounds warned her that someone was coming up the main stairway to the children's floor.

She relaxed as she saw Mademoiselle, clad now in a long green dressing gown, her hair in two braids, appear at the head of the stairs, turn there without pausing toward her own room.

Descending quickly, Dana watched the governess stop outside her bedroom door, press her forehead hard against the cool wood of the panel.

The wretched, interfering fool! Blind rage gripped Dana. Had the woman dared to go to her sitting room again, attempt to spy on her?

As Dana stood, her breath so indrawn that her small upper teeth pressed into her lower lip, Mademoiselle turned away, palms pressed to her temples, and went on down the corridor to the playroom. Obviously almost blind with pain or grief, she wavered across it to the double doors and stepped out into the darkness of the play porch.

32

Friday Morning, August 1

Under pressure of a hand on her arm and the urgent repetition of her name Dana roused from the deep sleep of exhaustion. "Dana! Wake up!" Carter Coyne's voice grew sharper.

She moved, forcing her eyes open, to look up vaguely into his dark anxious face. "Oh, it's you, darling. I thought—"

Smiling sleepily, she sat up, her eyes opening wider as she saw the room nacred with early-morning light. "Why, it's not day yet! Carter, what's the matter? The children—"

"They're all right. Dana, did you see Mademoiselle last night?"

"Mademoiselle! Last night?" She started, searched his face quickly, but it told her nothing. "Yes. Yes, she was here. She—she has one of her awful headaches. Last night—this morning sometime—she woke me to ask for some of my codeine tablets. Why?"

"She's dead."

"Dead?" Dana shook sleep from her quickly. "Dead! Not Mademoiselle—"

"She's dead," he repeated. "Here, put this on. And come quietly. I've carried her into the reception room."

With one foot in a slipper Dana looked up as if she had not heard correctly. "Reception— She isn't in her own room?"

"No. Don't talk. Come. Dock's here, I hope. I called him."

Wordlessly she followed him into the corridor, turned left behind him into the reception room. Its long length was bleak, eerily light as the picture windows on all sides revealed lawns wrapped in morning mist. Here and there firs and shrubs made dark blurs.

She shivered, stopped in the doorway. Her eyes traveled slowly about the room before pausing on the divan opposite the door, where Dock bent silently over a figure wrapped in a dark green robe.

He straightened, turned round as he heard Coyne behind him. For a moment the two men looked at one another blankly. Then Dock gestured toward the divan.

"You shouldn't have moved her, C. C. You know that, don't you?"

Coyne nodded. "I took a chance she might still be alive. And I didn't want one of the children to run out on the play porch, see her—"

Dana heard the words, but they held little meaning for her. Her eyes fixed on the white face with the dark shadow extending from the hairline halfway down the cheek. Not a shadow. A bruise!

"Dead for hours," Dock said tonelessly. "Everything on her is soaked with dew. Any idea what happened?"

"She's been working up a migraine headache for days," Coyne told him. "Dana says she came down last night sometime for codeine. Perhaps, unable to sleep, she wandered out on the play porch. Or she may have fainted—fallen—"

"Fallen?" Dana repeated. She did not move from the doorway. "Where?"

"I found her on the grass at the foot of the play-porch stairway." Coyne turned. "Come in, my dear. Sit down. You're all right?"

Dana nodded but did not move.

"She certainly struck her head a nasty blow on something," Dock declared. Pressing back the dark hair from Mademoiselle's forehead, he revealed the purple shadow that lay there also. Then, straightening, he caught up a folded silk scarf on the arm of the divan, shook it out, and spread it gently over the body. "That's all we can do now, I guess. I'll call an ambulance."

He led the way into the corridor, waited there until Coyne closed the door behind Dana. "Have you looked on the play porch, C. C.?"

"No. I'll do it now. Dana, see if Sardaki can make some coffee, will you?"

Dana sped ahead of the two, men, disappeared. Dock and Coyne stopped to look at one another again. Dock's face was white beneath its tan. Coyne's gray, the forehead ridged with deep lines. The eyes of both were tight and strained.

The younger man's lips twisted cynically, "And you want to buy Madison Farms!" he said and strode on.

In the living room they separated. Coyne vanished up the stairs. Dock turned to the telephone.

Ten or fifteen minutes later, when Coyne returned, Dock was sitting like an image in a deep chair, facing the beetle case over the fireplace. He did not look round when Coyne spoke to him.

"She must have tripped over a croquet mallet," Coyne was telling him. "The box is right there at the head of the stairway, and one mallet is lying across an upper step. Perhaps she started down in the darkness, fell over it—"

Dock rose stiffly. "It would be," he said.

Dana came in as he spoke, followed by Sardaki bearing a coffee tray. Obviously the cook knew nothing of Mademoiselle's death. Her beaming smile faded, however, as she looked from one to the other of the two men. She paused questioningly but, when no one spoke, placed the tray on a small table and left the room.

As Dana seated herself to pour the coffee Dock turned to the door. "None for me." He looked at Coyne. "I'll be home—if you want me."

Coyne remained standing until Dock's footsteps, echoing on the stones of the terrace, silenced suddenly on the grass. Then he drew a chair closer to the table, sat down heavily.

"I'm still in the market for Madison Farms," he told her.

Dana looked back at him with shadowed eyes. A faint shudder ran over her. "They're yours."

33

Friday Morning, August 1

Dad Madison brought Dana's deeds to the Farms to Coyne shortly after eleven. A serious-faced Ellen admitted him, seated him in the living room.

"Will you wait just a few minutes, Mr. Madison? Mr. Coyne's making a long-distance call."

"My daughter?"

"Mrs. Coyne's lying down, sir. In her rooms. The poor thing! She looks like a ghost."

"The children?"

"Doris took them over to spend the day with the twins right after breakfast. They don't know, sir. They think Mademoiselle got up early to go in to New York for a couple of days, as she sometimes did. They're all excited about what she'll bring them. It's terribly sad, isn't it? Shall I tell Mrs. Coyne you're here?"

Dad shook his head. "No. I'll wait for Mr. Coyne."

The maid looked at the shaken, old man, her eyes filled with pity. More than ever, she thought, he looked like a bit of thistledown. And no wonder, with all these awful things happening one after the other.

"Bad luck comes in threes," she wanted to assure him. "Bixby, Mary, and now Mademoiselle. There won't be anything more." But he appeared so sunk in sadness and despair, she thought better of it, went away.

Dad sat silent, his hands gripped tightly in his lap, looking at nothing, thinking of nothing. After a time in the stillness of the house he lifted his head. How long had he been sitting there? Faintly from behind the closed door of Coyne's sitting room he could hear a deep voice speaking.

The beetle case above the fireplace caught his eye. Sunlight and the dark bodies of Whiffles' beetles made the golden ones doubly brilliant. Almost the last thing Mademoiselle had done for the youngster, he remembered. Rising, he went over to look at it.

He was still standing there, rooted to the floor, his hands gripping the mantel, when Coyne opened his door. He came out, picking up a big brown envelope from the chair where Dad had sat. His gaze followed Dad's to the black beetle before he invited, "Come in, Dad. Sorry to keep you waiting. I've been trying to reach Mademoiselle's brother in Georgia. Just talked with him now."

With concern he watched Dad release his hold on the mantel, walk with a stumbling step, leaning heavily on his arm. He said no more until he guided the old man to a chair beside the massive glass-topped desk near his sitting-room windows.

"The brother wants her body sent to Georgia for burial," he continued then as he returned to close the door. "I caught Bowen at the station in Hanotak. He'll remain in town, make the arrangements before he returns. My lawyer'll have to come out by taxi."

Seating himself before the desk, he looked at Dad to see if he should talk longer. But the old man had pulled himself together. Somehow now, however, he seemed to have aged before Coyne's eyes. His glance was dim. He lifted a tremulous hand, rubbed it along the glass.

"I'm glad you're here, C. C.," he murmured, then began to pat his pockets worriedly.

"This what you're looking for?" Coyne touched the manila envelope. "I brought it in."

"Yes, that's it. Dana's deeds to the Farms."

Coyne's concern deepened. "You're taking this too hard, Dad," he cautioned. "I know you considered Mademoiselle a member of the family. To have her go like this—now—must be a great shock to you and Mother."

Dad raised his hand. "I must get back—to Mother." His voice was thin and dry to the breaking point. "The papers are all here."

But he made no move to rise, and Coyne waited patiently for the words he saw trembling on the old man's lips to take form.

"I—I'd like to talk about one more."

"One more?"

"The deed to our ten acres—Mother's and mine. I—I'd like to sell them to you too."

Coyne's voice was very gentle. "Why, Dad?"

The old man cleared his throat. "Well, we—we're getting along. Isn't much I can do now. And Mother—she don't throw things off as she used to. Mary's death rests very heavy on her. She feels responsible, though she has no right to. Now Mademoiselle—"

"But to sell your home—will that help her?" Coyne paused. "You don't mean you want to leave it!"

Dad nodded. "We—Mother and I—have heard about places—real nice places, with small private cottages in their own gardens—where old people like us can go. You—you sort of buy in, and you can live there the rest of your life. They—take care of everything."

He waited but, when Coyne waited, too, went on reluctantly, "We kind of want to lean back now, Mother and I. Have things peaceful. We don't need such a big house, ten acres of land."

Coyne's keen eyes studied the white, almost transparent profile, the twitching muscle at the corner of the pale lips. "How long since you and Mother Madison have had a holiday—a change from Madison Farms?" he asked finally.

"Don't know's I can say. Nine, ten years maybe."

"And since yesterday you've changed your minds about building up a breeding farm here with Dock and me?" Coyne asked after another silence.

"I guess you can handle that without me, C. C." Dad's voice was thinner still. His hands, laced together in his lap, showed ridges of white. "You were just talking yesterday. Including me—to make me feel good."

"I don't talk just to talk, Dad."

"No, I guess you don't. Fact is, I'm sorry to leave Madison Farms. Just when it looks as if they might get somewhere. I'm glad you're taking them over. Real pleased about it. We—Mother and I—hated to watch what Bixby was doing to them. And we'd hate to have a stranger get hold of them—while we're alive anyway. But—"

"But—?"

"Well, these last years have been a strain on Mother. She—I guess you'd call her an orthodox sort of woman. Likes to have things happen in an orthodox sort of way. Not that she wants to side-step her share of trouble. But it wears her down when our—when our deaths and taxes aren't like—like other people's. I figure it's worth more to me to have her unworried in a strange place than worried about strange things on our own place."

"She knows about selling your home? Agrees?"

"Well—no."

"What about Chang?"

Dad winced. "I—I don't know whether he can go with us or not. And I don't know what we'd do without him. Been with us twenty-five, maybe thirty, years. If we can't take him, Dock—"

Coyne's eyes were warm. Leaning over, he placed a steadying hand on the old man's shoulder. "Now let me do some talking, will you? I've just been waiting for a chance like this."

In the leisurely way he drew forward his chair no one would have guessed that the piles of letters, telegrams, and cables on his desk or the imminent arrival of his lawyer meant anything to him.

"I've got a ranch out West—two or three of them. This is the first of August. Wonderful time out there. How about you and Mother beginning the month right with a trip West? Stop off at the Mayo clinic in Minnesota on your way. Have a complete checkup, both of you. Chang, too."

At Dad's protesting gesture he smiled, went right on: "I've an idea you won't have to remain there long. Then if they say you can cross the mountains, go through the parks, Yellowstone, Glacier, whichever you like, and on to my Idaho ranch. If the mountains are too much for you, then my Montana ranch is just your dish."

Slyly he looked up beneath his heavy brows to catch Dad's expression, smiled to himself. "We're going to have the finest horse ranch in the East right here on Madison Farms. You and Dock and I. I'll bring men on from the West, of course, but I'll be away most of the time, and Dock will be busy with his victims. You'll have to serve as eyes for all of us."

Dad's eyes misted. "I believe you mean that," he said slowly, then shook his head. "It's impossible."

"Every word of it. And nothing is impossible. This is a business proposition. Requires study, thinking over. You can't say no until you've been out West, seen ranching there, can you?"

With a hand on the desk Dad pushed himself erect. "I—I'll have to talk with Mother."

"Of course. And send Chang over here. I'll tell him what to pack for you. Oh—I'm making Bowen superintendent here. He'll look after your house. You won't have to worry about a thing."

"I must talk to Mother—"

"Then it's settled. You'll go." Coyne opened the door, patted Dad on the shoulder. "These Madison women are tougher than you think, Dad."

34

Friday Afternoon, August 1

As the little group about the grave of Mary Bixby turned away Dock Madison touched Coyne's arm. "How about letting me drive you home, C. C.? Evoans is here and he's asked Daph to ride with him."

Coyne looked up into the young doctor's set face. "Why not?"

Until they had seen the big car on its way with Dana, Dad, and Mother Madison in a silent, white-faced row in the back seat, Dock did not speak again.

"My car's over here." He led Coyne to the small roadster across the highway from the cemetery, waved as Evoans' car with Daphne sped by. "Strike you that that fellow's out here pretty often? He called me early this morning from New York to lunch with him in Hanotak today."

"Anything new on his mind?" Coyne asked as he settled himself in the seat.

"There is now. I got the report on those analyses this morning. And you're right, C. C. That stain on the cotton checks with the analysis of Mary's blood and with—with Amery's."

"You mean you told Evoans that?"

"That and your whole theory about Bixby and the beetle." Dock put the car into gear. "Maybe we've been underestimating Evoans. At the time I thought we were both discussing the case, but while sitting through that service I realized he'd scraped my mind clean without telling me a thing himself. I'm sorry, C. C."

"No reason to be. He had to know sometime. He didn't tell you what he thought about my theory, about the analyses?"

"Just swallowed everything like so many oysters." Dock drove silently for a minute or two, then began again without preamble. "Hear you're sending Dad and Mother West—swell idea."

Coyne cocked an eyebrow slightly. "I'm no Evoans, Dock. You'll have to tell me yourself what's on your mind. I can see that something worries you."

Dock's lips twisted in a smile that had no humor. "I want to sell you my ten acres too, C. C. And I want to send Daphne and the twins away for a time, but I don't want you to offer to send them. I just wanted to tell you—first. They can go to the mountains or a lake for a month or so—while I look around for a new location."

Relieved to have that off his mind, Dock drew out his cigarette case, offered it to Coyne.

Coyne waved it away. "You don't have to explain anything to me, young fellow."

Dock lighted his cigarette, took a deep drag. "Mary's death—on the heels of her father's disappearance—isn't passing unnoticed, as you saw just now. On top of that, Mademoiselle's—"

"You mean that popeyed mob around the chapel just now? They'd have been out if we'd been displaying a two-headed calf."

"I mean Senator Amery particularly. He's been waiting—" Dock shrugged. "At the moment he isn't bothering me. But Daphne is. She can't take any more, and there's no reason why she should. And Mark and Matt have ears like circus tents. They range up and down the highway.

Know everyone, hear everything. They're bound to hear the gossip."

Coyne broke in on Dock's, incoherence bluntly. "Gossip isn't what's worrying you, son. For heaven's sake, stop this grasshopper and talk."

As Dock drew over to the side of the road, shut off the engine, Coyne eased himself round to say, "No, I will. And with gloves off."

Dock's answer was to fling away his cigarette.

"I'm all for your Mother and Dad having a change. If nothing had happened since I arrived here, I'd still be for it. People can't live in one another's laps as you all do here—without periodic changes of scene and faces and ideas. You need more freedom yourselves, And to give others more."

He smiled to himself at Dock's stern young face. "And I'm all for Daphne and the boys going away for the same reason. In fact, if you think they'd enjoy ranch life I'll be delighted— No? Be a lot more fun for Mark and Matt. I have one ranch that offers both mountains and lake. Trout streams too."

As Dock remained obdurate Coyne's voice changed. Anger glinted in his eyes. "Maybe you and Dad know more than I do about what's happening around here. Nothing happens without a cause, and certainly the cause of Bixby's disappearance dates back before we arrived last Sunday night. Yet I bought Madison Farms today—in spite of all that's happened. And now today you and Dad, to whom the Farms have been home all your lives, come to me, trying to get out from under.

"That sort of thing doesn't sit well with me. If you and Dad know a good reason today for selling your homes you must have known it yesterday. Yet you wait until the deeds are signed—and Dad until half an hour before—to speak. And then try to unload on me."

Dock stirred uncomfortably, moved to speak, thought better of it.

"I'm waiting for an explanation," Coyne told him. "I couldn't press Dad. But I can press you. In plain words, what's behind all this?"

Dark color stained Dock's tanned cheeks, but he merely sealed his lips more tightly.

Coyne pricked him again. "Looks like Dana's the best man in the family. You saw yourself this afternoon what a grip she had on herself. After all, what's happened here has touched her more than any of you. But she isn't trying to run away. To get out from under. What are you and Dad afraid of?"

Dock shifted his weight. "Nothing. I mean I've nothing to say. Except one thing, of course. My land is not for sale."

"Good." Coyne turned back in his seat impatiently. "Then what are we waiting for?"

Dock set the car in motion. They said no more until he stopped again before Coyne's door. Coyne stepped out, turned, smiling.

"Forget it, Dock. I will. And let me know later if Daphne and the boys would like to try ranch life."

Dock's eyes meeting Coyne's were dark and inscrutable. He nodded but could not speak. His own face inscrutable, Coyne watched him drive away.

Half an hour later, comfortable once more in his worn outdoor clothes, Coyne was on his way to the woods. After a time, by a roundabout route, he arrived at the east side of the slough that had once been Pelleas and Melisande. Although it looked more than ever like a stagnant swamp, he regarded it with satisfaction. As he pushed his way around it through the high dried grass he paused to study it from one angle and another.

The arsenical green surface, now about two feet lower, was one cause for his satisfaction. At this rate, he estimated, if no rain fell, a week should see the water almost completely drained away.

At length he reached the mass of stones and cement chunks with which Bixby had choked the little stream that once gave outlet to the pools. The continued dry weather had made of its shallow bed a depression in which stones, dead leaves, and branches discouraged a few hardy weeds from reaching the light.

As he looked down into it movement beneath the blackberry bushes beside him brought a smile to his face. "Hello, Bessie," he greeted the buxom and shining black snake that slithered out. "How's the hunting? Good, I take it, or you wouldn't be here."

Some sound too slight for Coyne's ears sent Bessie quickly on her way. Turning, Coyne looked up to see Hedrick parting the branches of trees on the bank.

"Good afternoon, Mr. Coyne," the violinist greeted him as he stepped down to the stones. "You don't mind my trespassing, I hope. My caretaker has left me little natural woods to ramble in. So I developed the habit of coming here."

"Not at all." Coyne smiled and waved a hand at the desolation around them. "If you want a change from your own place this should satisfy you."

He watched Hedrick move across the stones to look at the pond. As surprise, consternation flashed briefly in his face Coyne stepped to his side to look down too. Below them Bessie was winding a sinuous way toward the tall grass beyond.

"That's just a tame black snake," he explained. "I brought her over from Dad Madison's place to tidy up the rattlers."

"No, not the snake. The water. It's going down."

Coyne nodded, pleased. "You notice that, do you? Yes, Dad and I fixed up a makeshift drainage system, hooked up to the engine in our pump house." He nodded toward the right. "We're draining the water off there to flow through the east orchards. This dry weather, they can use it."

"You're going to drain the entire pond?"

"Might as well. The water's of no use here. Incidentally, I've a surprise for my wife up my sleeve. She used to have two pools here she thought a lot of. Bixby—her superintendent—ruined them with this rock pile."

"You're going to restore them?"

"Not right away, of course. Pretty late in the season to do much. But since the orchards need water, I can drain the place and help the trees at the same time. This fall I'll get rid of these stones and deepen the bed of the stream that ran here."

Hedrick turned slightly, an odd smile on his lips. "You have great energy, Mr. Coyne."

"Keeping busy's the best remedy I know for shaking off carking care," Coyne informed him gravely.

"Bixby's disappearance, his daughter's death weigh heavily on you?"

"Two women dead, a man's unexplained disappearance in less than a week don't come under the head of what I call recreation."

"Two?" Hedrick turned back, looked again over the pond.

"Mademoiselle—the children's governess—died last night. Fell down an outside stairway in the dark—"

Coyne's voice stopped. Hedrick did not answer. They stood silent on the brink of the stones, gazing unseeingly across the green surface to the enclosing woods. Although the sun shone brightly on only one patch of the stones, the heat here was oppressive, as tangible, as a weight. The silence was oppressive too. Except for gossamer winged insects darting over the pond, nothing moved.

At length Hedrick stirred to pat a folded handkerchief over his face and throat. "I beg your pardon, Mr. Coyne. I'm afraid I missed what you were saying. You were telling me your plans for this spot?"

"Was I?" Coyne took out a handkerchief, too, patted his face absently as he described his ideas for restoring the pools. "About halfway across this—swamp," he concluded, "there's a low dividing ridge. Tomorrow, maybe, you'll be able to see it. I believe my wife had ideas about building a bridge just there. With all that tough grass cleared away, the woods, too, cleared for paths, grass sown, flowers—well, by next summer this place should be something to see."

"Very interesting," the violinist assured him. "Perhaps I'm selfish—to prefer it to remain as it is." Obviously he had heard little, if anything, of what Coyne had said. With a glance at his watch he stepped back. "And now if you will permit, I must return." With a slight bow he turned for the bank.

"Of course. Come again whenever you wish."

Hedrick stopped, turned slowly round. "Thank you, but this is something like a farewell appearance. I'm leaving today—immediately—for New York, and then for—for a rest somewhere." His glance turned from Coyne's level gaze. "I've been working very hard—preparing to tour the camps and for my own concerts."

"Good luck to both," Coyne told him. "Though my wife will be sorry not to have seen you."

Hedrick hesitated. "She'll understand," he said finally. "She knows—my fiddle comes first."

35

Friday Afternoon, August 1

Coyne was sitting on a flat stone, putting the finishing touches on a small sketch in his notebook, when a hail from the road surprised him. He looked up to see Evoans coming down to the stones.

"Hi!" he greeted the agent. "Why didn't you send someone from the house to find me?"

Evoans smiled evasively, stopped beside him. "Nothing in particular on my mind. I came out this way really to see that fiddler across the road. Had a definite appointment with him. Not there. The chap's as elusive as an eel."

"Hedrick?" Coyne paused to study his sketch at arm's length. "He was here just a moment ago."

"He was? Where'd he go?"

Coyne looked up. "Take it easy," he advised. "Give him a chance to get home."

Evoans squatted on his heels to peer over Coyne's shoulder at the sketch, then eased himself down on the stones. "Oh well—probably just routine, seeing him, anyway. Boy, what a day! Though I don't call this the ideal place to spend it." He looked about at the matted enclosing woods and the pond. "Don't let me interrupt you—if you call that thing work."

"This?" Coyne held off the sketch again. "I call this work—and play. It relieves what I use for a mind. Funerals always get me down. This is an adaptation of the moon bridges I've seen in China. How do you think it will look there—about the middle—when this swamp becomes two pools again?"

Evoans wasn't raptly interested. "I hear you've just escaped another one. Funeral, I mean, in case you're listening. Mrs. Dock told me about Mademoiselle. You found her, she said. You didn't report it?"

"To the police? I don't suppose so. Clear case of accident. Dock took care of everything."

Evoans made no comment but took out a flattened packet of cigarettes, offered it to Coyne. When he had lighted their smokes he flicked the match idly over the pond. "Days like this I wish I were a farmer or a fisherman."

Coyne twinkled at him. "What could you do you aren't doing now?"

"Sit on a stone and *not* think." Evoans turned an open, almost ingenuous gaze on Coyne. "You see, sir, I'm new at this sort of thing—perhaps out beyond my depth. As you can imagine, the FBI in New York has a few important matters on its hands these days. I'm not a regular agent—just a private detective they sent down to investigate this Bixby and his rumor spreading. No one guessed it would develop into anything like this. And Bixby's the man I'm after—dead or alive. It's not my business to be concerned with anything else, yet I can't help thinking—"

"You're doing all right, young man, whomever you represent," Coyne told him, amused. "You're entitled to a rest while I tell you my ideas for this place. I've already given this lecture once—to Hedrick. Ought to be good now."

As Coyne described the scene before them as it would be, Evoans listened, his intelligent eyes on the desolation as it was. "So you're thinking of draining this frog pond," he commented when Coyne came to an end. "Not a bad idea. Not bad at all."

He sent the butt of his cigarette in a high arc over the green surface. "Now how about you listening to a few of my ideas?"

"Why should I?" Coyne chuckled. "I know damn well you didn't listen to mine."

"Because I can't get rid of the idea that Mademoiselle's death was no accident."

Coyne sent his cigarette after Evoans'. "I'm listening."

"How much do you know of her history?"

"Not much. Born in Belgium forty-two years ago. Educated there and in Germany. Lived or traveled a lot in Switzerland. Came to this country about seven years ago. Has a brother in Georgia. The rest of her family, if any, is still in Belgium. Mother Madison can tell you all about her."

"How much do you know about her and Bixby?"

"Dad and Dock both gave me pretty complete details on the way that clod pursued her. First with attentions: object, matrimony. Later with persecutions—anything to torment and humiliate her."

"Did she strike you as a woman to take that passively?"

When Coyne shook his head Evoans agreed. "Nor me. And I seem to know a thing or two you don't. One is that Mademoiselle's family was practically tops in Belgium—in Brussels—until the last war. She lost everything then, including a husband and child. She was also related—distantly—to Professor Fretz Dreier. And Dreier's no small-time name in Holland—or wasn't until the Nazis marched in."

"And the second thing?"

"Mrs. Dock told me this on the way out this afternoon. She says that when Whiffles was born Dreier sent for

Mademoiselle. Made her the nurse, practically the guardian of his son. I believe his will gives her the interest on what Whiffles inherits at twenty-one and specifies that Mademoiselle must remain with him."

Coyne nodded sagely. "For an FBI representative hunting a rumormonger, you've traveled far afield, haven't you? Anything about my own life you've had difficulty in uncovering?"

Momentarily Evoans was embarrassed. "Well, you see, sir, if, following up a simple assignment like Bixby, I can get to the bottom of what's going on around here—"

"You'll have a feather for the hat you seldom wear?"

"There'll be no feather for my hat—if I involve two men like you and Hedrick."

Coyne's eyes were shrewd now. "And you see in Mademoiselle's death a way to solve everything and leave Hedrick and me snowy white?"

"Yes sir." Evoans was serious now. "You see, I've been studying those three sets of analyses Dock showed me today—on Amery's death, on Mary's blood, and on the spot on the cotton. They all tell the same story. Rattlesnake venom. You expected that, didn't you?"

"And Dock told you, too, my theory about Bixby and the missing beetle?"

"Yes, and I've borrowed a lot of it—to complete an idea of my own. Based on Mademoiselle."

"You think Bixby had a hand in her death too?"

"On the contrary. I think Mademoiselle may have had a hand in Amery's death, in Bixby's disappearance or death—and Mary's."

"And her own?"

"Yes sir. You see, Mademoiselle was here much longer than Bixby. Under the Dreier regime, according to Mrs. Dock, she was practically the *grande dame* of

Madison Farms. And she was the only one who really knew and understood Professor Dreier's work. She knew all about that dehydrated preparation of rattlesnake venom he worked out and the reason why the Dutch government sent him those gold beetles for it. I believe that a little of that stuff goes a long way toward exterminating vermin in Dutch Guiana. And after Dreier's death Mademoiselle helped Mrs. Madison pack away his apparatus and personal things. She had opportunity to secure both the missing beetle and the venom."

Coyne's eyes, opaque now, fixed on Evoans' face. "Those analyses show that Amery and Mary did not die of undiluted natural venom? Is that what you're saying? And that Mademoiselle, not Bixby, secured it and the beetle and tried them first on Amery? In heaven's name what for?"

Evoans' eyes fixed on Coyne in surprise, then cleared. "No, perhaps you wouldn't know that. Mrs. Dock told me this afternoon. And I'm sorry to be the one to tell you now. But from the time Amery arrived here, relations between him and your—his—wife were strained. For one reason because almost immediately he tried to divert himself with Mademoiselle."

"Go on," Coyne ordered when he paused.

"Mrs. Dock says that it was during those first weeks Amery was here that Mademoiselle took on that protective coloring she has kept ever since. That tight way of pulling her hair back, plain dark dresses, and so on. Living in the same house with Amery, she couldn't avoid him. And she couldn't, by Dreier's will, and wouldn't, leave Whiffles."

"So—"

"On my way to find you this afternoon I stopped at your house, took a look at those gold beetles while Ellen was hunting for you. One could easily be concealed in a woman's hand. I suggest that Mademoiselle, to get rid of

Amery, filled one with venom, applied it to Amery's arm either before he entered the woods that day or meeting him there."

"And that proving successful, she tried it again on Bixby? Could be, but I wish she'd thought to do that before we arrived Sunday night."

"You go too fast, Mr. Coyne. I doubt if she used the beetle on Bixby. Or needed to—until the unexpected return of Mrs. Coyne. My idea is that Bixby, in some way, found the beetle. He may have known or at least suspected Mademoiselle's use of it, used his knowledge, when she wouldn't respond to his attentions, to threaten to expose her to Mrs. Coyne. Your wife, I believe, hasn't been entirely happy to have Mademoiselle here, tried, when Amery became interested in her, to send her away. Amery's death ended the need for that. But Mademoiselle may have feared that when Mrs. Coyne returned now to find the same situation repeated with Bixby she would make separation from Whiffles final."

Coyne was silent for a long minute. "If you're right your first reason seems more logical. Mademoiselle knew that Bixby had hurried to the house on Monday noon for some reason so urgent he wrote an impudent note."

"There's plenty to back up that idea. Mademoiselle's manner when I questioned her about Mrs. Coyne's whereabouts at five o'clock Monday afternoon. The fact that she went into the woods herself as soon as the children were in bed. To find her cane, she said. Its condition suggests that she found it—put it to hard use."

Disgustedly Evoans picked up a bit of stone, hurled it over the pond. "I guess I'm just talking after all, Mr. Coyne. May be nothing to this. If I could find just one concrete detail—anything—that would pin someone to a definite place at a definite time! I've got everything else I need to know."

Forgetful of the hard stones on which they sat, of the withdrawing sunlight, the two men were silent, each immersed in his own thoughts.

"And Mary?" Coyne said finally, looking up.

"I'm on thin ice there," Evoans admitted. "But Mrs. Dock says that Tuesday, when Mademoiselle brought the children there for luncheon, Mary telephoned to ask for her. The child was so excited or angry about something that Mrs. Dock could hardly understand her. And Mademoiselle when called to the phone, listened only a moment, then hung up and ran out of the house. She met Mary on the lawns, returned to the gatehouse with her, and remained some time. I don't know, of course, but I suspect Mary found something that led her to accuse the governess of being responsible for her father's disappearance."

"Arid Mademoiselle used the beetle on Mary?"

"No, I accept your theory that Mary found it, pricked and poisoned herself. Though if she hadn't, Mademoiselle, threatened again with separation from Whiffles, wouldn't have hesitated to use it, do you think?"

Coyne did not answer immediately. When he did he caught the detective off guard. "So I did the thinking for a large part of your theory. Who did the rest?"

"Mrs. Coyne." Evoans looked blank for a moment, then laughed. "I had quite a talk with your wife before I came out here."

He sprang up to pace restlessly about as Coyne, without comment, rose stiffly, dusting himself off.

Abruptly Evoans returned and stopped beside him. "But I have some ideas of my own, Mr. Coyne. I came here deliberately this afternoon—to see what it would require to drag this pond. I confess I didn't expect to find you here or know of your intention to drain it."

Coyne's smile returned. "That's better. I confess I don't appreciate young men half my age thinking they can pull wool over my eyes. Now what do you expect to find here? That concrete detail you're looking for?"

"Yes sir. Bixby's body."

36

Friday Evening, August 1

Silently Coyne walked back through the grounds with the agent, thoughtfully watched him stride down Madison Farms Road to disappear in the entrance of the private road to Hedley Farm. Then he turned homeward, stopping on the way at Dock's to see the children.

A flushed and hilarious Whiffles and Bunny greeted him from a small supper table laid on the screened porch. Mark and Matt had the worn and slightly noble look of men who sacrifice themselves in a righteous cause.

"Picnic!" Bunny shouted, banging a spoon.

"We don't have to go home yet, do we, Carter?" Whiffles demanded anxiously.

Daphne appeared with a tray of tall milk glasses. "Why not let them stay all night?"

"Why not?" hc agreed. "If Mark and Matt can take it, they can."

Daphne distributed the milk, then, slipping a hand through Coyne's arm, drew him out into her small garden. "They don't expect Mademoiselle back until tomorrow, so they're no trouble. In fact, this is something of a holiday for them."

She smiled up at him, her eyes bright. "Speaking of holidays, that reminds me. Dock told me of your invitation, C. C., and I'm accepting it. Though I'm not telling him—or the boys—until morning. They wouldn't sleep a wink."

"Good."

Her smile flickered out. After a moment she asked, "Would you like me to take Whiffles and Bunny along? If Dana agrees, of course," she added belatedly.

His appreciation was obvious, but he shook his head. "No. I've been having ideas too, Daphne. And you'll have your hands full."

Quickly he left her for Dahlia Walk, but there his steps slowed. Against the paling evening sky floods of sunset colors were flowing upward from the west to dye the highest clouds. Grounds and orchards, green and quiet, flower masses here and there were bright with light. Birds dipped and swooped in play over the orchards before returning to the woods for the night. But ahead his own home was dark and somber except for the kitchen wing, where windows made mirrors for the sunset.

As he walked down the corridor to the living room the emptiness and silence of the house pressed round him. He sighed with relief when he opened the door to his own rooms, stepped inside.

Ellen's almost breathless response to his bell gave evidence that the servants, too, were not unaware of that silence and emptiness. He could hear glass and ice tinkle on her tray as she hurried to his door. Saw her backward glance as she entered.

"I suppose this means Mrs. Coyne isn't joining me for a cocktail? Or dinner?" he said as she placed the tray on the table beside his reading chair.

"No sir. Mrs. Coyne is in the summer dining room, preparing for the dinner tomorrow night. She said she didn't want anything now—just a tray later. And she asked would you mind having your dinner here or in the breakfast room, sir?"

Ellen paused uneasily. "Mrs. Coyne shouldn't work like that, sir—though the dining room does look lovely. But she's so tired; she'll make herself ill."

"I'll see what I can do, Ellen. But wait a moment. I've an idea that will help her—if you'll help me with it."

"Of course, sir. About the children?"

"You've been thinking of them already? Good. Think you could take them into New York tomorrow morning early? Keep them amused and happy for a day or two?"

"Yes, I could do that, sir. I've taken children before to zoos and parks."

"Good. I'll telephone the Terrill, then, for my suite to be opened for you. Bowen can take you in and drive you wherever you want to go. Don't forget a few toy shops. And a pet shop or two, of course. And," he concluded, smiling, "if the youngsters begin to fret for Mademoiselle, tell them a big surprise is coming. Go as far as you like on that. I'll think of something to make it come true."

And, smiling, he watched Ellen go, but his face was inscrutable as he mixed his highball, carried it to a window. He stood a long time, watching the woods darken and the first stars appear.

Half an hour later, dressed in summer whites, he opened his door, stood listening. The unaccustomed sound of music—of a languorous tango—came softly across the short corridor from the dining room. With a stride he reached the double doors there, thrust them open.

The long room with tall windows at the end photographed itself instantly on his mind. Down the center ran a gleaming table which now resembled a miniature bazaar of Central and South American dolls, vividly lacquered gourds, straw animals, silver trinkets, and other crafts displayed on a brilliant Guatemalan textile. Midway stood a tiny artificial Christmas tree hung with shining baubles.

On buffet and side tables great pieces of Portuguese silver from Brazil waited for the tropical fruits Coyne had ordered. Bowls and openmouthed jars from Mexico and Peru waited, also, for their tropical flowers. Behind them on the walls were textiles, wooden mosaics and brilliant silks.

Coyne's eyes registered every detail but vaguely, for their whole attention was on the end of the room. There a low dais, covered now with vivid serapes, had been laid. Against the tall windows towered a tall symmetrical tree, bright with lights and silver tinsel. About it Mexican and Salvadoran baskets were filled to overflowing with gaily wrapped gifts. More packages banked the tree.

And against this barbarous riot of color, Dana, all in white, her fair hair shining in the lights, was startling. More startling because she was dancing, slowly, absorbedly, completely unaware of the man watching from the doors. Of other eyes, shocked and critical, peering through the slit of the slightly opened pantry door.

Abruptly Coyne moved forward, snapped off the radio. Dana stopped, regarding him for a moment without recognition. Then she smiled and, stepping down from the dais, hurried toward him.

"You would come, darling," she cried. "You're worse than a child. But I'm glad. I wanted you to see it. It's lovely, isn't it?"

She spun round, waving her hands toward the tree, the table, the decorations on the walls, then spun back to clasp her hands about his arm. "It's barbaric, but say you like it."

Coyne did not answer. Freeing his arm, he moved about the room, switching off the lights of the tree and the shaded wall candles. As he did so he saw the swinging door to the pantry fall into place.

"Carter! Darling, don't turn off the lights. I'm not finished."

"For tonight you are." In the light of the candles flickering down the long table he turned to face her. "This is no simple family-party arrangement, Dana. It's more than a couple of Christmases rolled into one. It's the setting for some mad plan in your mind. Before you go through with it I want to know what it is."

The gay light faded from her eyes. She looked round the room, then in sudden decision her head went up.

"You're right, darling. It is to be a great occasion. Tomorrow night celebrates my farewell to Madison Farms."

37

Friday Night, August 1

Coyne did not move. His grave, opaque gaze remained on her, unwavering. Under it she threw off her ingratiating manner like a scarf.

"Don't look at me like that! You said yourself you knew this moment would come sooner or later. Now it's come—sooner than I ever dreamed. Carter, I want my freedom."

"Why?"

"Because I want to leave you. That was our agreement, you remember. That whenever I wanted it I had only to ask."

"I remember our agreement, Dana. But in more specific terms. Civilization would hardly be civil today if a marriage could be dissolved every time a woman changed her mind."

"You refuse?"

"I haven't—yet."

Her smile flashed again. "Of course you haven't, darling. Why should you? I've given you a lot in the past weeks, haven't I? A home, a family, the Farms to play with. You'll hardly miss me."

"Yes, you've given me a home. But mine only by marriage, by a ceremony, I should say. If anyone leaves it, it should be Carter Coyne. And he's not leaving. Neither are you."

"It's not mine any longer. I sold the Farms to you today, remember?"

"When we separate the Farms return to you."

"I don't want them. I never want to see them again."

"And your children. Whiffles? Bunny?"

Her face paled, then sealed over.

"This is their home," she said finally, firmly. "They must remain here."

"Dana!" His voice was gentle but peremptory too. "You're not yourself tonight. You're saying words you don't mean, that you'll regret. Go to bed now. Sleep. We can talk tomorrow."

He turned to open the doors, but she was there before him, her back against them. "Answer me, Carter!"

"What do you want me to say?"

"I want you to agree to a divorce."

"My dear child—"

"I'm not your dear child. Stop treating me like one—like a trinket, a trifle, a toy."

"You've given me no reason to treat you as anything else. This hour is no exception."

"You refuse to give me a divorce?"

He looked at her levelly. "I didn't go into this marriage blindly, Dana. I foresaw—times like this—when against your own best interests you'd want your freedom. I made an agreement with you on one ground only—that if you ever found a younger man, someone you really loved, wished to marry, could be happy with when married, I'd free you. Are you telling me you've found that man?"

"No," she said after a moment. "No. I'm not telling you anything."

"Then my answer is no."

"You refuse?"

"I refuse."

"Then I'll divorce you."

"On what grounds?"

"Cruelty. Incompatibility. What does it matter?"

"You must prove it."

"Prove! You—you'd contest a divorce?"

"Naturally."

She gazed at him in amazement. "But I can't mean so much to you—you'd fight to keep me," she protested.

"You? No." He allowed his eyes to travel slowly from the shining cap of her hair to the toe of her shining slipper. "Other things mean more to me. The peace of mind of your mother and father. The future of Whiffles and Bunny. My own life."

She studied him again. "And if I said there was a man—a younger man—whom I love, wish to marry?"

"When there is we'll talk again."

"There is."

"And the man?"

"Isn't it enough that I tell you there is such a man?"

"No."

"What more do you want?"

"I want to see him, talk to him. To be sure he is the man you should marry." As she gazed at him, stiffening with anger, he added, "To be sure marriage is what he wants too."

She bit back the words forming on her lips.

"The man is Hedrick?"

Dana's eyes became opaque too. "I will not answer."

"The man is Hedrick?"

"Yes."

"You have seen him, then?"

"You know I have."

"He has asked you to marry him?"

"Of course."

"He has asked you to marry him?

"Yes, I tell you. Yes."

"You remember definitely the word 'marriage'?"

She stiffened, staring. Swiftly veiled her eyes again. Nodded.

Coyne laughed. "Until Hedrick himself recalls that detail my answer remains no."

She drew in her breath slowly. "What do you mean?"

"Hedrick has gone."

"Gone! Where?"

He shrugged.

"How do you know? You've seen him? I don't believe you!" Suspicion flashed in her face. "You did something—said something."

"On the contrary. I was most hospitable. Invited him to come here often."

Her hand closed hard on his arm. "You're not telling me everything. What happened?"

Calmly he released her hold. "Nothing. It was just a casual encounter. As you know, he likes to visit the pond occasionally. As a change from his own manicured grounds."

"If you expect me to believe you, tell me what happened."

Again he shrugged. "Well, he saw that I was draining the pond—using the water to irrigate the east orchards. That interested him considerably. So did the news of Mademoiselle's death. When he left he said that was his farewell visit, that he was leaving, probably would never return."

Deliberately she sealed her ears and mind against the implications in his words. "No more?" She moistened her lips. "I mean, he said no more?"

"Something about my wife understanding that with him his fiddle came first."

Dana stood before him, silent, cold and white as an icicle. His eyes impenetrable, he looked at her, then quietly opened the doors. She did not move. After a moment he stepped into the corridor, closed the doors between them.

38

Saturday Evening, August 2

It was almost seven when Coyne returned by taxi from Hanotak. He stepped wearily from the car, his face gray and lined with strain. At the house door he stood a moment, as if reluctant to enter, then turned the knob decisively. In the corridor Dana was running to meet him, a huge kitchen apron, tied about her neck, billowing round her.

"Darling!" She seized his arm, pressed close to him. "Oh, where have you been? I've been so worried—all day."

"Sardaki didn't give you my message?"

"That you'd taken the children into New York? Yes. That was thoughtful of you, Carter. But they've gone! The servants, I mean. Walked out—this morning. Every one of them. Because they saw me dancing last night, they said! I don't believe that was the reason. They just don't like the country—or the work of a dinner—"

Her words rippled into one another as she spoke in a high, tight voice and clung more firmly to his arm as he moved down the corridor.

"Look!" she cried in the living room, nodding to the bowls of fresh flowers. "I've done everything myself. The dinner too. You didn't think I could, did you? You'll see. It's all ready. Hurry and dress, darling, something cool. See—"

She jerked the bow of the apron strings to pull off her apron. "I'm just wearing this." Flinging the apron aside, she spun round to show him the simple white summer frock, sleeveless, backless.

Coyne stood in the middle of the room, his inscrutable face intent on her. When she turned back she stopped short, then moved closer.

"Carter! What is it? Tell me. I'm so frightened, uneasy. I've just been talking—to talk. I worked all day, too, to keep from thinking. Darling, don't look like that. You haven't said a word. And Mother hasn't phoned. Or Daphne. No one has come near the house."

"They're coming, Dana. In a few minutes. To say good-by."

"Good-by!" She stiffened, startled. "Where are they going?"

"Mother's taking Dad to Minnesota tonight—to the Mayo clinic. Daphne and the boys are going with them as far as Chicago, then on to Idaho."

"Dad!" Anxiety showed in her eyes, but relief too. "He's ill? Why didn't they—"

"Don't, Dana. Don't say any more. It's no use. Dock and I are getting them away before—"

"Carter! You're leaving me too. You don't want them to know. They'd never forgive me. Oh, darling, I was afraid of that. All day I've thought you wouldn't come back. Don't leave me. I was mad last night. Completely mad. But Rick's gone. I'll never see him again. Never think of him. We'll get new servants. Bring the children back. We'll begin again."

She raised her head, listening, as slow footsteps sounded on the terrace. Coyne hurried to the doors, held them open while Mother Madison, followed by Dad, entered.

"Mother!" Dana stood back, admiring. "How nice you look in street clothes. I haven't seen you dressed like that in years. And Dad! Angel, you're quite the man about town—"

"Dana!" Mother Madison interrupted through pale lips. "Oh, my baby! I don't want to leave you. It isn't right for us to go."

"Nonsense. Of course you must go. Dad would be lost without you. Don't worry. Carter and I will take care of Madison Farms. You'll see."

Dad shifted helplessly, looked at Coyne. "It's late, Mother. The taxi's already at Dock's—"

As he spoke the screen doors opened. Dock, his face flushed with worry, stepped in. "Oh, there you are. Mother, perhaps you and Dad can round up the boys while Daphne— They're so excited—"

Dana glanced at him, said quickly, "Run along, darlings. We won't say good-by."

She kissed her mother lightly, though her hands were firm on the older woman's arms, steadying her. Then her father. Linking her arms through theirs, then, she walked with them to the terrace.

"Have fun, angels. And don't worry. No tears, Mother. They—they make these stones so slippery. 'By, Dad. Luck to the heart. Keep it ticking."

Chattering as they moved away, she watched her mother grasp blindly for her father's hand, go on without turning. Behind her she heard Dock saying, "Evoans has just phoned. They're leaving Hanotak at seven-thirty. The Senator won't—"

"Won't wait, eh?" Coyne completed. "Well, that's that, son."

Dana did not change position, but the pupils of her eyes dilated until they appeared black. She entered the living room, letting the doors close slowly behind her.

Dock watched her steady steps toward them. "Good girl. You handled the parents just right." He stopped, added uncomfortably, "Dana, I'll have to say good-by for Daphne and the boys. She couldn't—"

"It's all right, Dock." Dana smiled up at him. "Run along yourself now. I want to talk to my husband."

Color surged to his face. Stooping, he kissed her hard. "I hate to go, C. C.," he said, turning away hastily. "I wouldn't—if there were anyone else to get that caravan on the train. I'll be back as soon as I can."

Dana and Coyne stood motionless until the doors slammed together behind him and his footsteps died away. Then she looked straight at him.

"Senator Amery is coming here? Why?"

"With Evoans. And others. He has an order for your arrest."

"My—!" She stood rigidly still. "Why?"

"They've found Bixby's body. Recovered it from the pond this morning." As thoughts raced across her dilated eyes he stopped.

"But the Senator—"

"Since the day Blake Amery died the Senator has believed he did not die accidentally. He employed Evoans to find proof."

"But Evoans is an FBI—"

"Only for this special assignment to investigate Bixby."

"They—know about Bixby?"

"About Bixby. Blake Amery. Mary. Mademoiselle."

Though her feet remained fixed to the floor, she rocked visibly at the mention of each name.

"They need only to prove that you—that one did not die a natural death, Dana. They can prove how Bixby died."

Slowly her tension relaxed. Her eyes lightened a little. "I can prove how he died too, Carter. I should have told—when Evoans first came. I—I did strike him with Mademoiselle's cane. But in self-defense. He stumbled—

fell into the—the pond. He just happened to come while I was there—"

"He didn't happen to come, Dana. He was there to meet you."

"Ridiculous!"

"It's no use, Dana. Evoans has Bixby's message which Mademoiselle left in the black beetle in the case. Dock found it—and knew. So did Dad. So did I."

"Mademoiselle! In the beetle?" She turned to look at the case. "It's gone!"

"Mademoiselle put it there—Thursday night. I saw her—just a few minutes before you came running down those stairs."

Gazing at him as if mesmerized, Dana's face drained slowly of life. "You knew! And Dad! Dock too. That's why—"

"Dock and I were thinking of you, also, Dana, in getting them away."

"But you—they—judged me unheard. On that insolent message," she cried angrily. "I—I had to kill Bixby. To save my own life. I can prove that—"

Coyne shook his head. "Dock and I spent hours with Evoans this afternoon. He has all the evidence he needs. All, Dana."

Gazing at him, a long shudder ran through her body. "Not Rick!"

"Evoans located him in New York last night. As he said and you must have learned years ago, Dana, with Hedrick, his violin comes first."

Unbelieving, she stood motionless. But there was no mistaking the truth of Coyne's words. At length she took a step toward him. Her voice was clear as she asked curiously, "And why are you here, Carter? Why didn't you leave me—with all the rest?"

His eyes held hers. "I remembered, trinket, the night we met in Buenos Aires."

She started, then swiftly understanding flooded her face.

"Sí, señor. I remember also. When I lost my last peso you offered to stake me for one more play. And I won."

"Muy bien, señora. But surely I did not step to your side, say, 'Here you are, lady.'"

Her slow smile matched his. Turning, without a word, she led the way to the dining room. In the doors she paused, her eyes darkening as she looked round the long table, now laid for the family fiesta. At the flowers and fruit in their bowls. At the tree and candles waiting to be lighted.

Stepping in, she took a packet of matches from an ash tray, coolly selected a match, struck it, and began to light the candles. For a moment Coyne watched her, a hint of admiration in his eyes. Then he turned to the portable bar standing ready at one side.

When he turned round, two cocktails in his hands, the candles were lighted. So was the Christmas tree. Framed against it, Dana sat in a tall-backed chair at the far end of the table.

He placed the cocktail in his right hand carefully before her, remained standing, the other in his hand. Slowly he lifted it. "To your next play, trinket."

Her fingers tightened about the stem of her glass, but she did not lift it. "The children—" she began, stopped as her voice trembled. When it was clear again she asked, "You'll keep them—for me? You won't let the Senator take Bunny?"

"The children are mine, Dana. I've already started adoption." Her head went back, and she studied him with clear, alert eyes. "You are the man who fights to keep what he wants, aren't you? You wanted my children, my family, my Farms. Carter, you gave the beetle and the message to Evoans!"

"Naturally." His voice was even, without emotion.

She leaned forward, trying, in the wavering light of the candles, to penetrate his dark gaze. "Because of Hedrick? Because of Hedrick! You said—you said you'd ruin me—and the man too!"

He stood motionless, still holding his glass to her, his eyes fixed on hers, waiting. "You need not accept my judgment, Dana."

She drew her glass closer, looked into it. "I choose yours, darling. But I won't suffer?"

"No. The heart stops instantly. A—a natural death, Dana."

"From Dock?" she asked.

He did not answer. She nodded, then looked about the long table waiting for its guests. "So the bride dines alone!"

She drew in her breath slowly, then, with amethyst eyes steadily on his, lifted her glass to her lips.

About the Author

Vera Kelsey (1892-1961) was the daughter of an American couple, born in Winnipeg, Ontario. She grew up in Grand Forks, North Dakota. She was a reporter for the *Fargo Forum,* and graduated from the University of North Dakota. Her early writing career included working for the *North China Daily News,* which allowed her to travel extensively in Asia, and then she spent almost five years in South America, particularly Brazil, before making her home in New York. She wrote mystery novels, travel books, and historical and regional nonfiction. She spent her last years in Minneapolis, and owned a cottage on Lake Minnetonka.

Coachwhip Publications

SATAN
HAS SIX
FINGERS

VERA KELSEY

CoachwhipBooks.com

Coachwhip Publications

CoachwhipBooks.com

Coachwhip Publications

CoachwhipBooks.com

BRUTAL
Question
by
OLIVER WELD BAYER
author of
"AN EYE FOR AN EYE"

The Serpentine Club Investigates
Murder in Washington, D.C.
THE CAPITAL
MURDER
JAMES Z. ALNER

THE
DARTMOUTH
MURDERS
THE
WAILING ROCK
MURDERS
CLIFFORD
ORR

SAMUEL ROGERS
YOU'LL BE
SORRY!
YOU LEAVE
ME COLD!

Coachwhip
Publications

www.ingramcontent.com/pod-product-compliance
Lightning Source LLC
LaVergne TN
LVHW091043080826
845145LV00002B/607

* 9 7 8 1 6 1 6 4 6 5 5 8 2 *